Stolen Innocence

Becoming Elena

book one

By

MELODY ANNE

STOLEN INNOCENCE
Becoming Elena: Book One

Copyright © 2016 Melody Anne

All rights reserved. Except for use in any review, the reproduction or utilization of this work in whole or in part in any form by any electronic, mechanical or other means, now known or hereafter invented, including xerography, photocopying and recording, or in any information storage or retrieval system, is forbidden without the written permission of the author.

This is a work of fiction. Names, characters, places and incidents are either the product of the author's imagination or are used fictitiously, and any resemblance to actual persons, living or dead, business establishments, events or locales is entirely coincidental.

ISBN-13: 978-1523259113
ISBN-10: 1523259116

Cover Art by Adam
Edited by Karen Lawson
Interior Design by Adam

www.melodyanne.com
Email: info@melodyanne.com

 /MelodyAnneAuthor  @AuthMelodyAnne

Second Edition
Printed in the USA

OTHER BOOKS BY MELODY ANNE

Billionaire Bachelors:
*The Billionaire Wins the Game
*The Billionaire's Dance
*The Billionaire Falls
*The Billionaire's Marriage Proposal
*Blackmailing the Billionaire
*Run Away Heiress
*The Billionaire's Final Stand

The Lost Andersons:
*Unexpected Treasure
*Hidden Treasure
*Holiday Treasure
*Priceless Treasure
*The Ultimate Treasure - **(December 13th, 2016)**

Baby for the Billionaire:
*The Tycoon's Revenge
*The Tycoon's Vacation
*The Tycoon's Proposal
*The Tycoon's Secret
*The Lost Tycoon

Surrender:
*Surrender - Book One
*Submit - Book Two
*Seduced - Book Three
*Scorched - Book Four

Forbidden Series:
*Bound -Book One
*Broken - Book Two
*Betrayed - Book Three
*Burned - Book Four

OTHER BOOKS BY MELODY ANNE (CONT.)

Unexpected Heroes:
*Her Unexpected Hero
*Who I am With You - Novella
*Her Hometown Hero
*Following Her - Novella
*Her Forever Hero
*Her Accidental Hero - **Coming Soon**

*Safe in His Arms - Novella - Baby, It's Cold Outside Anthology

The Billionaire Aviators:
*Turbulent Intentions
*Turbulent Desires

The Midnight Series:
*Midnight Fire
*Midnight Moon
*Midnight Storm
*Midnight Eclipse

Becoming Elena:
*Stolen Innocence
*Forever Lost
*New Desires

Collaborations:
*Taken by a Trillionaire
*Fall into Love
*7 Brides for 7 Brothers

Novels:
*Finding Forever

PROLOGUE

FOR FIFTEEN YEARS, Elena's life had been better — had been as close to perfect as she was allowed to have. She'd let go of her past and had embraced her present, had accepted who she was. She'd liked the person she'd become.

It had all been because of *him*.

Now she found herself leaning against the wall, wondering how she was still on her feet. The world was a cruel, cruel place and she had first-hand knowledge of that. Everything had come crashing down around her with no way of fixing it — not this time.

She'd been in love — as much as she was capable of feeling that foreign emotion. Maybe that wasn't what it was. It could very well have been need. But even if it was need, that was so much stronger an emotion than she normally felt. Elena wasn't a fool — she knew to care for anyone was extraordinary. It was even greater to have them care for her. She fell down to the floor, her legs no longer holding her up.

He had been hers for so long she wasn't sure she could live without him. In a ball she laid there. Not too many people knew her story. She'd covered it up well, was respected, owned a business, and had a husband — not that he was worth mentioning.

Those she was closest to would be shocked by her choices in life. They wouldn't care there was a reason she was who she was. They would just hate her — call her a monster — call her a whore. One of the few women she'd actually called *friend* had discovered her most coveted secret this very night — had walked into the room while Elena had been begging her previous lover to take her back.

The woman — her friend — had vanquished her from her life and the life of her son though *he* was a grown man and could have chosen to stay with her. But even if her friend hadn't vanquished her, *his* girlfriend, who claimed to love him, had already done so. The money-greedy bitch. She couldn't love *him* like Elena did. She didn't understand *him* — didn't have a clue how to handle the pain he'd suffered.

Elena had taken his hand, had guided him through his nightmares, had taught him how to deal with them, how to deal with life. She'd been the one to heal him, had been the person there for him when he'd needed it most. She'd held him, whipped him, and made love to him in every conceivable way. And he'd chosen that naïve little girl over her. If it hadn't been for Elena *he* never would have been whole enough to be in a relationship with her. But instead of thanking Elena, the girl had taken *him* away.

That chapter was closed so tightly she would never be able to fix it this time. She couldn't believe she'd lost *him*. She could barely breathe she was so upset.

The pain was too much. It was too much.

Elena had been through hell and back. But through it all, she'd managed to survive. She wasn't sure she'd survive this, though. She'd needed *him* and he'd moved on.

She and *him* had been the perfect match from the moment their eyes had met — both of them filled with so much pain no one else could possibly understand. She'd recognized it in him and she had known she couldn't turn away from what had to be done.

From that moment on the two of them had been one. Elena didn't care if the rest of the world looked down upon their relationship — she had always known it was pure, it was love, it was extraordinary.

But it was over. She had lost *him*. It had all been for nothing. Everything she'd ever done that had led her to this point had been for nothing. Elena hung her head, unmoving as she gave up on it all.

Without *him*, she had no will to carry on.

CHAPTER ONE

Fifteen Years Earlier

SITTING ON HER little brother's bed, Mary gave Tommy a gentle smile as he bounced up and down in excitement, his hands cupped before him, a huge grin showing the whiteness of his teeth.

"Come on, Sissy, I can't wait," he said with a giggle.

She placed a box in his hands, and his eyes shot open as he looked at the bright green wrapped package with a white satin bow on top.

"What is it?" he asked as his seven-year-old fingers reverently trailed across the ribbon.

"You'll have to open it to find out," she told him with a laugh.

Carefully, unlike most seven-year-olds, he slid the bow off and undid the tape, not wanting to tear the wrapping. She knew he would save it, as he saved all his wrapping. It was an odd habit, but she sort of liked that he did it. It was only one of the many things that made Tommy unique.

When the box was open, he pulled out a journal with a compass and his name etched on the front, with a pencil attached to the side.

"Wow," he said, his fingers rubbing over the raised lettering. "This is my name."

"I know you want action figures and pellet guns, but I wanted to give you something that makes you think of me when I'm away at college," she told him.

"Why do you have to leave?" he asked for about the hundredth time, his eyes swimming with tears.

"I'm going to a university. Besides, this house is too small, and it will be easier on Mom when she's not feeding four mouths."

"Mom loves us both," Tommy insisted.

"Yes, I know she loves me just as much as she loves you, but I'm graduating high school soon and I'll be a grown-up. This is what grown-ups do," she tried to explain. "And see that compass on the front cover? If you put your hand on that and close your eyes and think about me, you will know I'm out there, and I'm thinking about you," she assured him.

"I just don't want you to leave," Tommy said as he carefully set the package down and curled up on her lap, something he'd done since he had been crawling around on the floor as a five-month-old.

Their mother and Mary's stepfather, Dave, both worked full-time, so Mary had always spent a lot of time with her little brother. Sometimes, she was frustrated when she had to babysit instead of going out with her friends, but most of the time she didn't mind. She loved Tommy, even if she hadn't been thrilled when her mother had first married Dave.

It wasn't that Dave was horrible or anything. He was mostly indifferent to her. She would rather have that, than have him come in and try to act like her father. No one could replace her dad; she wouldn't allow it.

He'd died when she was only eight, but she still remembered how he would rush in the door after work and pick her up, giving her a kiss on the forehead before spinning her in a circle. He'd always told her she was the most important person in the world to him. She was his princess.

His death had left her empty. But she and her mother had eventually begun to heal. And then Dave had come into the picture. Mary was glad that Dave made her mom happy, but he drank a lot, and he was lazy, in Mary's humble opinion.

Her mother did everything. Worked full-time, cleaned the house, cooked, came to all of Mary's school functions. When her mother had gotten pregnant with Tommy, Mary had been worried. Because that meant even more changes.

But from the moment her little brother had been born, she'd cherished him. And he'd bonded with Mary. She really did adore the kid.

"You have to come home and see me a lot," Tommy insisted. "Promise me!"

She held up her hand, her pinky sticking out. "I promise."

They locked their pinkies together, and then she leaned forward and kissed his cheek.

A pinkie swear could never be broken. It was the most sacred of oaths in her opinion.

But sometimes, the promise was taken out of a person's hands. Sometimes their feet were swept out from beneath them. And sometimes promises were broken . . .

CHAPTER TWO

THE NOISE WAS driving her insane! Mary loved her little brother — his friends she could do without. And her stepfather insisting she play all the little kid games was making it even worse. She needed freedom, and she needed it now.

Grabbing a rose from the vase of flowers sitting on the dining room table, Mary plucked a petal off and moaned.

"What's the matter?" her mother asked with an indulgent smile.

"I need to get out of here," Mary grumbled.

"I told you I don't like you walking when it's late, especially now with snow on the ground," her mother said, a hand on her hip.

"You also know I have to take a walk each night — rain or shine — or I feel like the walls are closing in on me," Mary countered, gripping the long stem tightly in her fingers.

Her mom sighed as she gave Mary a once-over. Before she said anything, Mary knew the battle was over.

"Don't be out late."

"I won't."

With a roll of her eyes, Mary walked from her front door with a huge sigh of relief. Sometimes she wondered if her mother and stepfather realized she was nearly seventeen. Probably not, since they treated her like she was Tommy's age.

She'd been trapped in the house all day with her little brother's friends who were spending the night for his birthday. Her mother had insisted she celebrate with the family. She'd already had her moment with Tommy that morning. She didn't need to stick around and play with first graders.

Alone time was most certainly a necessity at the moment. Besides, Mary had always loved to walk. She lived in a very small town in Iowa. Nothing much ever happened, so she didn't see why her parents, especially her mother's husband, had to be so dang strict all the time.

When that man laid down the law, her mother tended to fall in line. She'd been walking this road for years. He could get over trying to instill more rules. She had a little over a year to go and then she was out of there. If it weren't for Tommy, she would be so relieved to get away that she probably wouldn't even come back home at Christmas.

Already feeling calmer the farther she got from the house, Mary smiled as she noticed a couple birds chirping on the ice covered power line.

As she moved through the packed snow, she dropped petals from the red rose on the ground, leaving a trail behind her. When she turned and saw the beauty of red against the crisp white powder, it made her smile. Home could be boring at times, but it also could be peaceful and filled with so much beauty there weren't adequate words to explain it.

She continued walking as the sun lowered in the sky. She'd have to turn soon, but not yet. She wanted to reach the old power plant first. That would be a solid three-mile round-trip walk. She tugged her jacket a little bit tighter against her chest and kept on plugging forward.

When she heard tires on the crunchy snow behind her, Mary jumped, quickly spinning her head around and nearly slipping on the icy ground. There wasn't a lot of traffic on this backcountry road, but there was plenty of room for any vehicle to get around her. She spotted a large black SUV pulling up behind her and felt her first stirrings of unease. She quickened her pace.

"Hey!" someone yelled. She ignored him.

"Stop please. I need directions," the person continued. She slowed her pace and then turned around.

The person speaking looked to be only a few years older than she was. Not threatening at all. She weighed her options. She didn't trust strangers. But she also lived in a small town where you helped your neighbors.

"Where are you trying to get to?" she asked, not moving back toward the guy.

"It's up on Territorial I think. The address is smudged, but I have this map here," he said with a sheepish laugh.

Mary smiled. Yep, it was most likely some city slicker who didn't have a clue how to navigate country roads. Of course it was. No one in her small town as young as him would be driving an Escalade. That was a rich man's car. The teenagers lucky enough to get a car in her town drove old beat-up Ford pickups, and they liked them.

Rust added character, and if the vehicle had four different rims, that gave the person bonus points. Mary wondered how she was going to fare at a college in a city. She was a country girl, and she was a little bit afraid she wouldn't fit in with a crowd of people who drove vehicles like the one this guy was leaning on.

"Okay, let me look at the map," she said, finally moving toward him. He was out of the SUV, after all, and he had the map laid out on the hood.

"I really appreciate this. Are you from here?" he asked, his teeth chattering just a bit, making him appear even more charming.

As she got closer, she saw he couldn't be more than twenty at most. Not terrifying in the least. He was actually kind of cute. She brushed back her hair and wished she weren't wearing sweats and a hoodie. The last of her worries fell away. She was a track star. It wouldn't be difficult to run away if she felt she were in danger. But cute guys weren't dangerous, she assured herself.

"Yes, born and raised," she said with a depreciating laugh. As much as she mocked the city slickers, she wouldn't mind living in a big metropolitan area herself. It sure would be better than cow tipping as a Saturday night activity.

"Very cool. I've never been here before," he said with a laugh. "Obviously."

She laughed with him as she leaned over the top of the SUV and looked at the map.

"How old is this thing?" she asked, trying to focus past the faded lines. She leaned in closer to get a better view.

"Just old enough," he said.

She picked up on the shift in his tone a moment too late. Suddenly there was intense pain in her head as something struck her on the back of the head. She didn't even have time to scream before the world went dark.

CHAPTER THREE

MARY CAME TO with a start. Immediately she sat up and swung around, trying to get her bearings. What was going on? Where was she? What had happened?

It was dark, too dark for her eyes to adjust, but as she squinted, trying to focus, she noticed a tiny bit of light coming in through a small window. She tried calming herself — not easy to do when she was petrified.

Slowly, her confined space came into focus. She was on a musty cot in a room where she could reach across and touch the other wall. The stench of urine, sweat, and other odors she was afraid to put a name to, drifted easily up her nostrils, making her gag. To top off all of that, her head was throbbing, and she desperately needed to use the bathroom.

But Mary was afraid to make a sound. She closed her eyes and tried thinking back. She'd been talking to the guy on the side of the road, then there had been extreme pain in her head before everything went black.

He had to have hit her, or he'd had someone else there; she hadn't seen who had hit her. But why? She couldn't figure that part out. If they had wanted to kill her, what was she doing in this musty room? She lay there for several moments as every bad scenario flashed through her mind.

She didn't want to contemplate what the man — or men — had in store for her. She was almost seventeen. She wasn't a fool. And right now, she thought death would be a better option than what might be coming her way.

Tears began falling from her closed eyelids, leaving wet trails on her dirty cheeks. She wasn't sure how much time had passed with her unconscious, but she knew it was enough that her mother was surely panicked, wondering where she was. And Tommy would be so upset. She'd promised to play a game of tag with him later that night.

"Mama . . ." she quietly sobbed, wondering why she'd been so mean the entire day. At this moment she'd give anything to hang out with Tommy and his friends.

Suddenly the door was wrenched open and light flooded into the tiny room, a man standing there in the opening.

"Good. You're awake."

Mary whimpered as he quickly approached, reaching out with gnarled fingers, harshly pulling her to her feet before she had even the smallest chance of slinking away from him.

"Please, I don't want to be here," she cried, his fingers bruising her skin.

"Yeah, well, life sucks," he answered with a chuckle before jerking her forward.

She lost her footing and fell to her knees, but he just yanked her back up, nearly pulling her shoulder from its socket. Pain shot through her body as he dragged her down a narrow hallway and up a set of squeaky stairs.

When they came out at the top, bright light invaded her eyes and several men were sitting around a table, two of them smoking, all of them holding a beer as they leered at her. She looked around, but the one who'd grabbed her was nowhere to be seen.

She didn't expect someone who drove such a nice vehicle to hang out in a filthy place like this, but where had he gone? She was trying to keep it together as she looked around for a weapon or a way to escape.

If they thought she was going down without a fight, they'd picked the wrong girl. But the odds of five to one didn't stack up in her favor.

"Are you sure we have to give this one up? I wouldn't mind keeping her for myself," one of the men said, his front tooth missing, his face unshaven.

"The boss already knows about her. So if you value your life, you'll keep your hands off," the man holding her snapped.

"I just want a little taste," the first man said as he stood and circled her, lifting his yellowed fingers and rubbing her cheek. She jerked away and gagged, which made the men laugh.

His tobacco and whiskey flavored breath rushed up her nostrils as he grabbed the back of her neck and pressed his disgusting lips against hers, his hand slapping her backside in a harsh crack.

She cried out, but that just made it possible for him to cram his tongue inside her cheek. She gagged again as bile rose in her throat, and he finally pulled back.

"Oh, yeah, I really want to keep this one," he said as he undid the top button of his pants and slid his fingers inside, looking like he was stroking himself in front of all of them. No one even blinked at his horrific behavior.

"I said she's spoken for. You do anything other than what you just did and you know the boss will kill us," he said. But he looked down at her with a similar look as he lifted a hand. "It really is too bad, though. She's real pretty."

Shaking where she stood, Mary refused to shed more tears as she glared at the man.

"Where are we? I demand to know where you're planning on taking me."

"Keep your damn mouth shut," the man snarled before raising his other hand and backhanding her, making her vision blur for a moment as she tasted blood in her mouth. She'd rather taste blood than his vile spit.

"No! I want to know where I am," she shouted back, struggling with the man still holding tightly to her arms. He wasn't releasing her, but as soon as the man who'd kissed her leaned forward again, she spit in his face, not caring about the consequences.

Fury rushed into his dark eyes as he glared at her with such hatred, she would have taken a step backward if she had been able.

His hand flew out and sharp pain slammed through her as he punched her hard in the chest, taking her breath away as she slumped down. Though she tried to hold herself together, the slight whimper escaping showed the group she was hurt and that made the ones sitting around the table laugh boisterously.

"I've got to get her ready," the man holding her said as he began marching her forward once again.

"I'll take over," another man from the table offered with a hopeful expression.

"Not going to happen," the obvious leader said.

She stumbled in front of him as he exited the kitchen and entered a dirty bathroom. The commode was covered in grime, the toilet paper wet, and the counter full of dirt. The sink and tub looked as if both hadn't ever been scrubbed. She recoiled from the smell alone — which unbelievably was worse than the bedroom she'd been pulled out of.

"Are the accommodations not to your liking, Princess?" the man asked with a harsh laugh. "You have two minutes. I'd use them wisely, because they will be your last. We're traveling for a very long time tonight."

He walked away from the door but didn't shut it. She saw his shadow in the hallway and knew he was standing right there. She'd either wet her pants or attempt to use the facility. As quickly as possible, and pulling her pants down only minimally, she hovered over the toilet and quickly did her business before she refastened her clothes.

The man was standing in the doorway when she looked up, an evil leer on his lips.

"It sure is a bummer to let you get away," he said as his eyes traveled across her young body.

She fought the tears wanting to fall. She wasn't going to give this man or any of the others anything else to laugh at. She would find a means to get away even if it was the last thing she ever did.

It wasn't just herself she was thinking about, either. It might be easier to give up if that were the case. But no. She had a promise to keep for her brother and one way or the other she was determined to do just that.

CHAPTER FOUR

MARY WAS BLINDFOLDED and tied up before being forced from the house and down a set of stairs. She was trying to remember everything she could, trying to hear the sounds around her, listening for anything that might give her a clue as to where she was.

She heard the rustling of trees, and the crunching of leaves. But not being able to see made it impossible for her to take in any clues to where she was. It truly seemed hopeless, not that she was going to give up so easily.

Before she could get her bearings, she heard a creaky door open and then she was pushed forward. She was lifted, and then the man was laying her down. She began to fight against him, but his fist connected with her jaw, nearly making her lose consciousness again as pain shot through her, and more blood oozed into her mouth.

She heard something above her snap shut, causing more fear to rush through her. Reaching her tied hands up, she discovered a solid wall above her. She reached to each side and found the same. She kicked out and there was nothing but walls.

Beginning to panic, she twisted from side to side as she tried to free herself. She was closed in completely. They must have placed her in a box — or possibly her own grave.

Her breathing came in pants as she struggled to free herself, but it was no use. Desperately she wiggled around until she didn't have the energy to struggle any further. She couldn't hear a sound. Whatever they'd put her in seemed to be soundproof.

But then she felt the vibration of movement. She stopped struggling and tried to pay attention. There was a bump of some sort and then just vibrating movement. She realized she must be in a box inside of a vehicle.

Okay, this wasn't good, but it didn't appear as if she were being buried alive — at least not yet. And thinking back, the man had said she was for someone. If that were the case, then surely they weren't going to be dropping her into the ground.

Although she might actually welcome death right now, she didn't want to die slowly, painfully, as she lost all oxygen or her body starved. She'd rather it went quickly so she could just sink into oblivion.

Mary slipped in and out of sleep as the hours slowly passed. She had no idea how much time had gone by, but when the lid to her box opened and a dim light shone above her, she took her first deep breath since she'd been placed in the soundless contraption.

"Welcome to your new home," the man said, an evil grin accompanying his words.

"Where's home?" she tentatively asked.

"Haven't you learned your lesson about asking questions?" he answered, reaching in and grabbing her hair, yanking her up to her feet.

It felt as if thick strands were being pulled from her head, but this time she didn't give him the satisfaction of tears. He seemed disappointed. He pulled her from the box, and she had only a moment to look at the tiny contraption her body had been crammed into before she was being yanked to the ground.

"Move it."

She fell to her knees when she tried to take a step. She'd been constricted in the tiny box for hours, and she couldn't walk. She tried standing and once again couldn't get back up. She didn't know what they expected from her. They were the ones who had entrapped her.

He gripped her arm again and dragged her forward. Finally her feet shuffled the tiniest bit, tingling shooting up her legs. None of the other men were around. She was somewhat grateful for that. But then again, what might this man try if he were the only one with her? She didn't want to find out.

"You're late."

The voice speaking wasn't one she'd heard before. It was almost formal, not as cruel as the other voices, but just as cold.

"I'm sorry. We had to wait until we knew the roads were clear," her captor said. "They put out a search on this one real quick."

"The boss doesn't like excuses." Then the man stepped forward and gave her an assessing look. "She's been beaten."

"She got a little out of hand, and I was forced to correct her," the man said.

"You know better than to touch the merchandise. The boss won't like this." A shiver traveled down Mary's spine as the new man looked her in the eyes for the first time. He circled around her, and the other man's hand fell away.

Mary thought for a moment about running, but as if the man knew, his lip turned up the slightest bit.

"Running will only get you injured," he said, his tone almost gentle. She found herself wanting to plead with him, beg him to let her go. He seemed as if he would understand.

"Please . . ." Her voice cracked on the one word.

"I'm just doing my job, little one. I can't do anything about it," the man said, his tone still soothing.

He then handed her captor an envelope, which the man opened before giving the well-dressed man a grin.

"It's a pleasure, as always, doing business with you," he said before he turned and walked away.

"Am I going to have trouble with you?" the well-dressed man asked.

Mary shook her head as she looked around. They were in the woods. Another van — this one much nicer — was parked about fifty feet away. It appeared as if it were only her and this new man. She was wrenching on the ties binding her hands. If she could just get them loose, she had a fair chance of getting away. She was sure she could outrun this man who appeared to be in his forties.

"I want to go home," she said when the ties didn't loosen.

"You are home now," he told her.

It was just the two of them, or so she thought.

"What in the hell is taking so long, Leo?" another voice called out.

"We're just getting to know each other, Rico," Leo responded, not taking his eyes off her.

The other man, Rico, approached, his eyes deadly cold. Mary found herself taking a step closer to Leo, who seemed to be the lesser of the two evils.

"She's trouble. I can always tell the troublemakers," Rico said with a grin, as if he enjoyed conflict. "Leo, get her secured. We still have a long way to go."

Mary's shoulders sagged. There was no way she was escaping both of these men. It didn't mean she wouldn't try if she had the chance. It just meant she was going to be hauled into another vehicle for now.

Rico grabbed her arm roughly and began tugging her toward the van.

"Please . . . I have to go to the bathroom," she said as he opened the back door.

"There aren't facilities out here," Rico said, his tone giving nothing away as to what he was thinking.

"I really have to go," she pleaded.

"Let her go. But I wouldn't let her out of your sight. This one's a runner. I can feel it," Leo said with a smile.

"Got it, boss," Rico replied. She was surprised. She'd thought Rico was the boss by the way he was acting.

Rico pulled her twenty feet away to a tree, in view of both men.

"Can I please just have a little privacy?" she attempted.

"You have one minute to get this done," Rico said.

"But my hands are tied. I can't get my pants down."

"Then I guess you're out of luck. You now have fifty seconds." The man looked at the watch on his wrist.

She knew he wasn't bluffing. She wiggled out of her sweatpants, doing the best she could with them both watching, humiliating herself even more. She quickly relieved herself before she pulled her pants back up, feeling disgusted.

"Let's go," Rico said as he glanced at his watch again.

Rico gripped her arm again and moved her to the van. Inside the back was a bench. The driver's area was caged off. She couldn't see past the wall separating it from the back.

Rico left her at the back with Leo then climbed in on the driver's side. Leo pushed her inside and then sat her on the bench. He reached for her ties, and Mary thought this might be the moment she could run. But before the thought was halfway out of her brain, the back doors sealed them in, and as soon as her ties were off, Leo grabbed one hand, threw a handcuff on it, and clipped it to the bar.

"We have a bit of a ride, so I wouldn't pull on that arm," Leo said as he leaned back, looking as if this were no more than another day at the office.

"Thanks," she sarcastically replied.

She knew it could earn her another slap, but she was furious.

Instead of the man striking out in anger, he laughed. "I think the boss will really enjoy you," he said, grinning at her.

"What does your boss want from me?" she asked after several minutes of silence. She wanted to know, yet she didn't. Although she would much rather be informed than not.

"It's what he does," Leo said with a sigh as he ran a hand over his face.

"What does he do?" she asked.

"He likes young girls," Leo said.

"What kind of monster is he?" she gasped.

"He's a very wealthy man who pretty much gets anything he wants," Leo told her. "If you don't fight this, just do what he wants, it'll be a lot less painful for you."

"Fight what? I don't even know what I'm fighting," she screamed.

"You know what this is about. The sooner you accept it, the better off you'll be," he told her.

"Please don't do this. I made a promise to my brother. I need to get back to him," she said, finally caving in to the tears again.

"I'm just doing my job," Leo told her.

"No, you're not!" she screamed. "You're kidnapping and abusing."

"Most people don't enjoy their work. They just do it," he said again.

"You're just as big a monster as your boss," she told him.

"I can be." The look in his eyes frightened her. She'd thought for a moment she had an ally in him. But it appeared she didn't. She had no one.

She didn't say anything else. What good would it do her anyway? Terror was sealing her throat.

She would escape. Mary was sure of it. She wouldn't let these people destroy her. She had a promise to keep. When the drugs they gave her kicked in and she began fading into sleep, she was grateful. She would get away from this reality any way she could.

CHAPTER FIVE

A BLINDFOLD WAS THRUST over Mary's eyes, and she didn't even fight it this time. During the entire drive, which had been hours upon hours, she'd nodded off a couple times with her head hitting the back of the van and causing her to wake up in a panic, unable to move her arms.

Leo stopped talking to her, and she refused to look at him, even when the van stopped and the men pushed her out to relieve herself again. She wasn't as mortified this time with someone watching her. Maybe she was just growing numb to it.

But when the blindfold slipped off just as the sun was rising in the sky, she knew they'd reached their destination, wherever that might be. She was terrified, but she also realized this wasn't going to be an easy escape.

Did that mean she wasn't going to try to get away at the first opportunity she got? Of course not. She would do anything in her power to keep the promise to her little brother, to go back home. But she also knew the choice wasn't hers right now. The situation was completely out of her control.

"This way," Leo said.

She stubbornly planted her feet and refused to move. It was like asking a mouse to run into the cat's mouth. How foolish did they think she was?

"Come on, little girl. You've been such a model prisoner so far," Rico said with a laugh as he nudged her back.

"Go to hell," Mary told him. She spit in the general direction she thought he was standing.

When he cursed, she knew she'd hit him. The slap against the side of her face, setting her ears ringing, also let her know he didn't appreciate her act of rebellion.

"Get this bitch inside before I knock out a few teeth," Rico growled.

"Calm down. That's not the worst substance you've had on your shoe," Leo said with a chuckle.

Mary was hefted into the air, and her breath rushed out when her stomach connected with Leo's massive shoulder, her head now dangling behind his back.

His hand trailed along her butt before he gave it a pat that infuriated her all the more.

"Be a good little girl," he said, the humor still in his voice.

"You can go to hell, too," she said, wishing she could be a lot more creative with her insults.

But even if she were acting tough, she was terrified. She didn't know what awaited her inside the walls of wherever they were taking her, but she knew it wasn't anything good.

Struggling against Leo's back only earned her another slap on the butt, this one harder, her cheek stinging beneath the cotton of her pants. She clamped her teeth together to keep from screaming out and earning more punishment.

When she was finally set down, she didn't move an inch. Her hands were still cuffed and the blindfold remained in place. She wasn't sure if she wanted it taken off. That would thrust her into the reality of all that was going on.

Mary wasn't sure she was ready for that.

She kept her eyes tightly closed as the blindfold was removed. She was in denial. If she refused to open her eyes, then the situation wasn't really happening to her.

"Open your eyes, little girl," Leo said.

"My name is Mary!" she finally screamed. She was sick of being called little girl.

"Not for long it isn't," Leo said.

Her heart stopped in her chest before resuming frantically. What was that supposed to mean? One thing she knew for sure — she wasn't ready to find out.

CHAPTER SIX

THIS TIME WHEN Mary woke up, the new room wasn't musty or as dark. It was slightly bigger but no more luxurious. She was once again on a cot, but this one had a sheet on it.

And there was an identical cot right across from her, within touching distance, but it was currently empty. As she pulled herself from her grogginess, she looked down.

She was horrified to see she was wearing a nightgown. The smell of shampoo hung in the air and, as she reached down and felt her legs, she could tell the grime was gone. She'd been cleaned. Someone had bathed her.

The tears she'd refused to shed earlier instantly filled her eyes and spilled over. She had been violated. She didn't know how far it had extended, but someone had stripped her, seen her naked, touched her.

The thought was terrifying and demoralizing.

Before she was able to put thoughts to words, the door opened. She cowered in the corner of the bed as a new man filled the entrance, stepped aside, and a young woman walked through.

Her hair was down, but clean, her clothing the same type of pajamas Mary was wearing. There was a decided slowness about her approach, and she didn't make eye contact with Mary.

"See you tonight, Patty," the man said before shutting the door. The distinct sound of a lock clicking echoed through the small walls of their prison.

"Where am I?" Mary asked. She was still cowered in the corner of her bed, holding her legs.

The young woman sat down and assumed the same pose as Mary, hugging her knees tightly to her chest as she looked over. Mary was barely able to see the girl's expression; the room was so dim. But what she could see was terrifying. It was almost as if an endless void rested within her eyes.

Mary shivered as the young girl trembled in the bed next to her.

"Please talk to me," Mary whispered.

The girl finally turned her head, making eye contact. Her eyes were deader than Mary had originally thought, devoid of all emotion.

"I'm Patty," she finally whispered.

"Patty, what is this place?" Mary asked.

"Hell," Patty replied.

"How do we get out?" She was feeling more panicked by the minute.

"We don't." Then there was a spark in her eyes as her gaze bored into Mary's. "Don't fight them. It will only make it worse."

Her words sent terror through Mary's body. She hadn't thought it was possible to feel more frightened than she already was, but those words had done it.

"Where am I? What do they want?" Mary finally whispered.

"You're here for the master of the house," she said, and then shuddered. "He wants you. He wants us all. One is never enough."

At the end of her sentence the words trailed off into almost nothingness. What had been done to this girl to make her talk this way? Mary couldn't imagine the horrors that were coming her way.

"I don't understand."

The girl in the bed next to her continued to tremble as she looked at her with a sad knowingness that Mary didn't want to see.

"You can't possibly understand. I didn't. None of us did." She said this with so little emotion that a chill rushed down Mary's spine.

"Please just tell me. You're frightening me more than I already am," Mary pleaded.

"I shouldn't have asked. It didn't help to know. I think that's why they room us together for a little while though. I think they want us to tell each other. They say to only speak positively. They say they are always listening, but really, there's nothing else they can do to us that they haven't already done," she began.

"What do you mean?" Mary wanted to scream, but somehow she kept her voice quiet. "How long have you been here?"

"I've been here for years." There was barely any inflection in her voice. "Four long years." Then she looked up, her eyes suddenly alert. "What's your name? How old are you?"

The intensity of her words made Mary flinch. She'd been showing such little emotion up to that point.

"I'm almost seventeen. My name's Mary," she said.

The girl gave an almost smile as she looked at Mary.

"I'm nineteen now. I was fifteen when I was brought here." Then her eyes went intense again, and she reached over and gripped Mary's arm.

Her arm was still sore from the first man who had pawed her, but she didn't tug against the hold. It was almost soothing to have this girl touch her, just to know she wasn't alone.

"Don't forget who you are. They will try to make you forget but don't. Remember," she whispered harshly. "Tell yourself every single day who you really are and when your birthday is. You will lose track of time. You will get sick and you will hurt, but don't forget. It's the only thing that will keep your feet on the ground — that will keep you from going insane."

She finished her impassioned speech and then let go of Mary and sat back again, her eyes going back to the lifeless slits they'd been when she'd first entered the room.

"What are they going to do to me?" She hadn't wanted to ask that question, but still, she had to know.

"Anything they want," she replied before taking a deep breath. "Some girls have it easier than others and some — the ones the master chooses, the ones like me — we have it the worst."

"What does he do to you?" Mary asked as she pushed back her newly formed tears.

"Everything!" she whispered harshly. "He's cruel and gets off on that," she said as a single tear tracked down her face, and she angrily wiped it away. "But if you fight them, it's worse. Don't forget who you are, but make them believe you've forgotten. The torture will stop being so harsh once they think they've broken you. But don't give in too quickly or they will know. They will punish you for lying to them. They don't allow us to lie to them. They don't allow us to think. They only allow us to do their bidding," she finished.

"I'm scared," Mary told her.

"I can't tell you not to be. Just pray the master doesn't want you right away. Hope and pray you have some time. I had a year before he took me. He was satisfied with the last girl before that. But then one day he wanted me." Another shudder passed through her.

"What happened to her?" Mary asked. She was trembling as she sunk down on her small cot and curled into a ball while still looking at Patty.

"I don't know. She was just gone one day." Patty lay down and faced Mary.

"Do you think they let her go?" Maybe Mary would get out of here.

"I have to believe that. She did what they asked of her. She truly believed she was who they told her she was," she said, her eyes bright. "Maybe they let her go."

Patty didn't sound as if she truly believed that. Mary couldn't fathom never seeing her family again. She couldn't believe how petty her thoughts had been when she'd last left her house. She'd do anything just to rush into her mother's warm embrace right now and tell her how much she loved and appreciated her. She'd really love to hold her little brother, smell his sweet fine hair. She'd never defy her stepfather again if she got to go home. She made all of these promises and more to herself in the hopes of escape.

"I really want my mom," Mary finally said.

"You can't think that way. It will slowly kill you if you do," Patty told her.

"How long were you with the other girl?" Mary asked.

"Only a couple months. They usually only put us with the new girls for a few weeks. I think they believe it will make us more cooperative. The more you make them think you're coming around to their way, the more rewards you will get," Patty told her.

Mary didn't know whether to believe her or not. Was this all part of the game to these twisted people? Was Patty a plant meant to comfort her?

Did it even matter? Mary didn't want to be alone right now. Even if Patty wasn't who she said she was, Mary still didn't want to be alone. The darkness, the fear, was all too much when she had only herself for company.

"I'll be good," Mary said, not sure who she was saying it to.

"Just don't give in so quickly that they know you're faking it. I tried that . . ." She shuddered as she held up her arm and showed the scar running down it.

"What happened?" Mary gasped.

"It doesn't matter. Just don't let them know you're trying to fool them. It won't go well for you."

Maybe Mary didn't want to know. The girl turned away from her and faced the wall, holding her thin blanket over her head as she began humming. Mary lay there and tried to figure out the tune the girl was singing, but she couldn't.

When the noise stopped and the girl's breathing evened out, Mary began to count sheep. She didn't know when they were coming for her, but it did her no good to try to stay awake. At least in slumber she could forget for a short time that her life would never be the same again.

CHAPTER SEVEN

A BLACK HOOD WAS thrown over her head while men yelled. Mary swung her arms as she tried to fight off her attackers, but it didn't matter. There were commands issued: stand up, face front, stop moving. Names were called, all while she was violently thrust forward.

Her knees trembled as her shoulder hit a wall, and then she tripped over a ledge of some sort. She couldn't see. Reaching out her arms, she tried to feel her way, but even that was taken from her when her hands were roughly jerked behind her back and secured with what felt like coarse rope.

"This way," a man growled as he yanked on her hand so hard, it felt as if her arm was going to be ripped from her shoulder socket.

She'd been left alone for two days and nights. Patty hadn't returned in that time, and all sorts of horrible things had flashed through her mind. The waiting was almost worse than the torture they were currently putting her through.

The hood was still secured over her head, the band almost too tight on her neck, when her clothing was ripped from her body. The cool air touched her skin, making her shiver as she waited for the worst.

When cool water began pouring over her head, she screamed. With the hood over her face, she felt like she was drowning. Shaking her head, she struggled against the binds at her back while trying to kick out, trying to get away.

More laughter accompanied her struggles as hands moved across her body, and the smell of soap hung in the air. When rough hands spread her legs, and every inch of her was scrubbed, she stopped fighting, pain shooting up in her stomach from their menacing touch.

Hanging her head forward, she tried to take shallow breaths, but even doing that, some of the moisture from the overhead water spray got into her mouth, making her still feel as if she were drowning.

Finally, the hood was ripped off as the water cascaded down her head before hands tugged on her thick strands, lathering them up.

There were four men surrounding her, shirtless as they took turns scrubbing her body and head and began shaving every inch of hair from her. She stood trembling, the men keeping her still as they talked amongst themselves as if she were nothing more than a statue.

"Damn, this one is my favorite I think," one of the men said as his hand moved down the front of her body before scrubbing her chest almost raw.

"I know. It's been a couple years since we've had a new one. I was wondering if the old man was losing interest," another man said with a chuckle.

"I'm damn glad he isn't," the third man called out as he began rinsing her hair.

"At least we get the leftovers. This one might just be worth the wait."

"Don't forget we get to play with her for quite a while first."

"Yeah, but only so much," one of the men said with a frown.

"Does he know she's here yet?" the quiet one asked as he stood directly in front of her, his face only inches from her own.

"Yeah, he does," another said.

"Too bad," the man standing in front of her said as he lifted a hand and cupped the back of her neck, leaning a bit closer so his lips were nearly touching hers.

Mary gagged at the thought of what they were going to do to her.

"I think she's a virgin. But maybe the boss would never know," the man said before his lips ran across hers.

"He always knows. Remember what happened to Joe when he decided to test that theory," the man behind her said, and the man in front of her released her lips and stepped back.

"Yeah. She's not worth that," the man said. "Almost, but not quite."

Looking into her eyes while he stood back, the man began undoing his pants as the guy behind her finished washing her head and gripped her arms, holding her in place.

She whimpered when the man in front of her pulled out his member and began stroking it. The other men laughed. She turned her head, and a tear slipped out as she closed her eyes.

"You need to watch this, little girl, see what's coming for you," the man behind her whispered before his tongue traced her ear and he pressed himself against her naked backside.

The other two men simply leaned against the wall and watched the scene play out.

"Open your eyes," the guy facing her, demanded. She shook her head.

The man behind her reached a hand up to her neck and squeezed hard, making her eyes fly open as she gasped.

"Keep them open or this is going to get a lot worse for you," the man behind her growled.

Tears streaming down her cheeks, she watched as the man in front of her stroked himself while reaching up and gripping her between the legs, the pressure sending pain into her stomach again.

"Damn, this would be better inside her," the man groaned as he continued stroking himself, faster and faster while his fingers nearly rubbed her skin raw.

"The boss says we can do anything *but* that," the man behind her said while tugging against her bound hands and continuing to lick on her ear before moving to bite her neck.

The tears stopped as she tried to take herself to another place, tried to picture being back at home where all she'd had to worry about was getting her homework done.

The man in front of her threw his head back as his fingers clamped hard on her core, making her scream out in pain. After what seemed like forever, he shook as he relieved himself on the shower floor.

It was quiet for a few seconds, then he pulled up his wet shorts and smiled while looking at the men against the wall.

"Who's next?"

He took the place of the man behind her as the torture continued while all four men relieved themselves, groping her, making her skin raw, making her bleed as they scratched and bit at her.

When it was over, they finished cleaning her before taking her back to the room, naked, and tossing her inside. She fell to her knees on the floor but didn't feel any pain. She stayed right there, trembling as tear after tear washed down her face.

The other girl was right. This was hell. Mary just didn't understand what she'd done so wrong in her life that she'd been thrust into the deepest pit of the abyss.

CHAPTER EIGHT

"YOU NEED TO get up off the floor."
The words came to Mary through a tunnel as she shook on the cold ground. She recognized the voice as Leo's, but she didn't care. She had only been in this place a few days and she already felt broken. She wished they would've just killed her in the beginning.

She wasn't even an adult yet, and the world had been so vast and exciting just a week before. Her biggest worries had been which college she wanted to attend and what she was going to choose for dinner. She'd thought life had been hard before she'd been captured. It didn't even compare to what she was going through now.

Her mother was gone, and the chances of seeing her little brother again, went down a little bit more with each minute that passed. This might just be the life she had to accept now. It might be it for her.

"You need to get up now," Leo said again.

She felt his hands grasping her beneath her arms and then she was lifted up and being carried to her bed. She wanted to tell him to stop — to leave her where she was, but she didn't even have the strength to protest.

"Come on, little one. I know this isn't ideal, but it can be a lot better for you if you don't fight it," Leo told her.

He pulled the covers over her, then gently rubbed her head. Mary couldn't keep the tears in as the gesture reminded her so much of all the times her mother had done the exact same thing when she wasn't feeling well, or when her heart had been broken for some reason or other.

"Please stop," she told him.

"Okay." He pulled his hand away. Mary was so shocked he'd actually listened to her that she looked at him. He gazed at her with sympathy, which she didn't know what to do with.

"Let me go home," she pleaded with him.

He looked down at her with an unreadable expression in his eyes. She wasn't sure what to do with that. For a moment she felt hope, though. Maybe he could save her.

"I can't," he said, before turning away.

"Yes, you can. I know you want to be a better person than this."

He sighed. "Once you step into this life, there's nothing that can be done. I'm here for the duration," he told her.

"Please, Leo, please let me go home," she said, reaching for him.

He clasped her fingers in a comforting gesture and squeezed. Then he let go and stood up.

"It's going to be hard for a while, but it will get better," he told her as he opened her bedroom door.

"Don't leave me like this. I just want to go home," she said, urgency in her tone.

He shook his head, but this time he didn't turn to look at her. She knew beyond a doubt that she'd lost this plea. He might want to help her, but he wouldn't. It was up to her to get out of this mess. No one was going to be her savior.

The room was even more silent than usual as she lay there for hours. Not a noise could be heard through the thick walls, and she wondered what was happening with Patty, or if there were other girls out there who'd gone through worse than she had. She wondered what was going to become of her.

Patty had told her to hold on to who she truly was, but that seemed almost impossible. She was so alone and so scared. Why had this happened to her? She wasn't a monster, hadn't been that bratty of a child. She'd just been a normal girl, living a normal life. Why her?

Sleep finally came to Mary, but not before she sobbed every tear out, and said several prayers for freedom. She would find a way to escape. It would be the one desire she held onto no matter what these people chose to do to her.

CHAPTER NINE

THE SOUND OF the whip cutting through the air was the only warning before pain singed across Mary's back. After only a week, she was learning to suppress the cries wanting to escape her lips. The more she cried out, the more they liked it. And the more pleasure they took in hurting her, the more intense the pain became.

Each day was something new. No one had spoken to her in what felt like forever. They spoke around her, or at her, but no one spoke to her. She wasn't allowed to speak. If she spoke, something sharp would be jabbed into her mouth, leaving her tongue raw and her lips bleeding.

She'd learned quickly to keep quiet. Often, tears would fall, but that would be the only emotion showing on her motionless body. It had taken days for her not to jump at the crack of the whip, a swinging board, or raging fists.

Her body was bruised and raw. Her mind was blank. She tried desperately each and every time they pulled her from her room, to go to another place, but it wasn't so easy to do when her aching body was the only thing she could focus on.

Escape.

That was the one word that flashed through her brain most often. If she ever gave up the hope of escaping, she would give up completely. It was what she wanted to do, what she needed to do. She wanted so badly to get away from these people, from this hell she was barely surviving.

They fed her, but it wasn't much. She was given a couple pieces of bread a day, sometimes with meat in it, sometimes just dry. She was lucky when she had juice to drink. That was when her body wouldn't stay upright no matter how many ties were on her. Most of the time it was just enough nourishment to keep her from dying.

She slept a minimum of twelve hours a day. Anytime she was in her room, that's all she did, before she'd be cruelly woken to endure hours upon hours of torture. She hadn't met the master of the house, had no idea what all this abuse was for.

The whip flew through the air again, this time crossing her chest, the end snapping at her bare nipple. The pain nearly made her pass out as she saw stars float before her eyes.

"That's enough for the day," Buster (she now knew their names) told the other men.

"My arm's worn out anyway," Rock said.

"You guys take the night off. I'll take care of her," Leo told them.

She almost perked up at the familiar voice.

She'd only seen him once since the night he'd carried her into her new prison — that night he'd comforted her before walking away. Why did she care? She didn't, she decided when the other men put away their "tools" and trotted from the room, talking about dinner plans.

Her stomach rumbled. She sat still, her arms beyond aching as they were held tautly behind her back with ties.

Leo stepped in front of her, and his eyes seemed kind as he looked at her. "How are you holding up?" he asked.

She looked at him without a clue of what he was expecting from her. She was never asked questions. If she spoke she was punished, so she just sat there, wondering if this was a whole new form of torture.

He lifted his hand and cupped her cheek, and the kind gesture almost undid her. She so needed someone to care about her. But this had to be another ploy, and he was going to lift that hand in a moment and slap the cheek he was currently caressing. He was just as bad as the rest of them.

"I know this isn't easy. I know your life has been taken from you. But the hard stuff will pass," he said, standing and going behind her to loosen the ties.

When her hands were unbound they flopped beside her in the chair. She still didn't move. She didn't do anything without being told anymore. Even if she found an opportunity to escape, she was so weak she didn't think she'd be able to get away. Not unless she had plenty of time to crawl for miles and miles.

Leo moved around to the front of the chair and undid her legs, then he scooped her up into his big arms and moved to the bathroom. Mary didn't enjoy the cold showers. They weren't freezing, but the water was never more than tepid. She would often wake hours later after getting back to her room, her body still shaking, unable to get warm.

Leo sat her on the toilet, and she didn't try to hide herself. What was the point? All the men had touched her, abused her, and stripped her of her dignity. She didn't think of her body as hers anymore.

Leo started a bath, and she turned her head the slightest bit. They normally threw her in the shower. Sometimes it was quick, sometimes excruciatingly long, but they never gave her a bath.

Her body instantly began to shiver as she anticipated being submerged into the cold water. She could handle it, she told herself. It wasn't any worse than what she'd already been through.

When Leo lifted her and sat her in the water, her eyes widened, connecting with his gaze. The temperature was bordering on too warm, but she wouldn't complain. It felt too good on her aching muscles.

"How does this feel?" he asked as he picked up a sponge and added a nice dollop of soap to it.

She still didn't respond. He was asking her a direct question, but she hadn't been allowed to speak for so long, she again didn't know if this was another trick. When his hand moved toward her, she couldn't cover up the flinch. He stopped.

"I'm not going to hurt you right now. I'm going to clean you up, get you a nice meal, and then leave you alone," he told her.

He didn't move until she finally nodded her head.

Pushing her forward so she was hugging her knees in the hot water, he began rubbing the soft sponge over her back. The contrast of his gentleness was unnerving because she was no longer used to it.

He said nothing more as he gently scrubbed her entire body, being more careful around her severely bruised places. When he was finished, he had her lie back, washed her hair, helped her stand, and then turned on the shower and rinsed her off.

When she stepped out, he held a fluffy pink robe open and a small sigh escaped Mary's lips when he wrapped it around her. She quickly clamped her teeth together, afraid she was going to get in trouble for the sound.

"It's okay. I know you've been put through hell. That's just the process, little one. If you just quit fighting this, it does get easier, I promise," he assured her and placed a hand behind her back, leading her to her room. She wasn't fighting anyone. She was in no shape to do that. So what in the world was he talking about? She wanted to ask, but didn't dare do it.

"I'll be back with food," he told her before shutting the door.

She waited but didn't hear the latch connecting, telling her the lock was securely in place. She moved to the door, and her fingers caressed the knob. Was this a test? Was he on the other side waiting to see if she tried to run?

She gripped the doorknob, her fingers trembling as she tried to decide what to do. When her knees began shaking she knew even if it wasn't a test she was in no shape to run. What if she got past this dungeon? She had no idea where to go, how to escape the house, or even if there were guards.

If it was a test, she wanted to pass it. She needed them to believe she was accepting her fate. The more they trusted her, the better chance she had of getting away.

Slowly, she moved over to her bed and sat, then pushed back against the wall and pulled the covers up around her. With the hot bath, thick robe and her cover, she was warm for the first time in a week.

Her eyelids began to droop, but she fought it, hoping Leo hadn't been lying, that he was bringing her food right now.

When the doorknob turned, she looked at the opening with wariness. Just because Leo had said he was bringing her food, didn't mean that's what was happening. This could all just be a pause in the torture. They might want to make her comfortable before they began beating her all over again.

When Leo's face smiled in at her, and the smell from the tray drifted across the small room, she began shaking again. He set the tray on her lap and sat across from her as she looked down at the cut-up steak, macaroni and cheese, bread and butter, and full glass of milk. She was afraid she was going to wake up any minute and the food would be nothing but a dream.

"Dig in before it gets cold," Leo urged her.

She didn't hesitate any longer. She gulped the food down, not looking up as Leo laughed. All too soon, the entire plate was cleaned, the milk emptied.

Leo stood and took the tray.

"Not everything or everyone here is bad," he told her as he cupped her cheek. "Not all of us are the enemy."

"You're the one who brought me here," she told him.

He sighed, shifting on his feet. "I've never felt as badly about it as I have with you," he told her.

"Why?" She was growing braver with him being so nice to her. She might live to regret it.

He looked at her for several moments, his fingers twitching against the tray. She took the time to study him. He was younger than the other men, probably about twenty-five. She wasn't exactly sure. He had brown eyes and dark hair and his lips rarely smiled. He was so large he was scary, and she wondered if this was the only job he'd ever had. She wanted to know why he would do it if it made him so unhappy.

"Maybe I've just seen too much and I don't want to see it anymore," he told her.

"So then help me," she pleaded with him again, though it hadn't done her any good so far.

"I can't," he said.

He then turned and walked from the room. This time she didn't feel as hopeless though. This time, she felt like maybe there was a chance it would get better. With a full stomach and a warm body, the aches were barely noticeable; Mary lay down and swiftly fell asleep. Maybe tomorrow wouldn't be as bad a day . . .

CHAPTER TEN

ELENA WOKE, FEELING confused, and for a moment she forgot where she was. Stretching out her arms, a smile flitted over her mouth before it evaporated and she panicked thinking about the math final she had to take.

Opening her eyes, she sat up, and then the fog cleared as she looked around the tiny room she was imprisoned in. Darkness surrounded her, but she could still see the faint outline of the bed next to hers and the light sneaking beneath the closed door.

Footsteps were her only warning before her door was thrust open and three of her captors walked in with varying expressions. Leo seemed subdued as her eyes connected with his. Rico obviously enjoyed his job a little too much, and Rock was the clear leader of the group — the most vicious of them all.

"Blindfold her."

This was a new voice, and somehow it sent a shiver of fear through her unlike anything else had done so far. Rico stepped forward, his hot breath on her neck, making her stomach turn. Her hands were bound before she knew what was happening and then the light went out as a cloth was placed over her eyes. Not being able to see made the fear grow even more intense.

"Done boss," Rico said.

More footsteps could be heard and then she felt more hot breath on her face as if someone were close, examining her in the most personal of ways. She tried to struggle, but Rico was sitting behind her, holding her in place.

A hand ran down her body and she shook as tears dripped down her face. What was going to happen to her now? Each moment that went by meant the chances of escape were less and less.

"I want to go home," she sobbed.

The man in front of her gripped her neck and squeezed so hard she lost her breath. Her throat hurt when he released her and Mary decided it was best not to say anything as these men surrounded her.

"Let me make it very clear to you," the new voice said. "This *is* your home."

He didn't sound angry — there was actually very little emotion in his tone. But that made it so much worse. He spoke with finality and confidence. He'd done this before and he had no doubt his commands would be followed. Why weren't the others afraid of her seeing them, but he wouldn't allow it? It made her wonder who he was that his identity had to be kept secret.

"How is her training going?" the man asked.

"She's a stubborn one," Rock said.

"Then it will be a while before the master will see her," the man said. Mary almost let out a breath of relief. This wasn't the master, the one who they were preparing her for. Then maybe that meant she had more time.

"Do you have anything in mind?" Rock asked.

"You know what to do. No scars," the man said. The bed shifted and she felt his weight leave as he stood. He said nothing else before he walked out the door.

The blindfold was taken from her eyes and it took a few moments before her eyes adjusted, and then she looked from Rock to Rico and then sent a pleading glance to Leo, who looked away. She wanted to scream at him. Why didn't he help her? Why didn't he do something if he hated what was happening to her?

"Are you ready?" Rock asked. Looking into that man's eyes was like staring at a black hole. They were void of anything but ugliness. He was nothing more than an animal and she was sure he hunted anything he considered weaker than him. He didn't do it for the sport either, he did it to feel superior. She wanted to call him out on it, tell him he was a jerk, that he could burn in hell for all she cared. She didn't say any of that, though.

Rock moved out of her line of sight and Mary felt more fear. She never knew when the pain would come to her when she couldn't see them. If they were in front of her, at least she had a little bit of warning. His fingers landed on the back of her neck and he squeezed, making her skin crawl. She bit her bottom lip as she waited to see what was coming next.

"Please …" she said, not even knowing what she was pleading for. It fell on deaf ears, but she couldn't seem to stop herself.

"Yes, I like that pleading tone to your voice," Rock said as his fingers moved to her cheeks and he caressed her. She tensed. Then he reached behind her and undid her restraints.

Her wrists pulsed as the blood flowed back into her tingling fingers. She wasn't so foolish as to try to get up, to try to push any of the men away. That would only lead to more pain for her.

Rock stood and walked to her door. He didn't turn back around. "Bring her to the training room," he ordered, and then he was gone.

Mary looked again at Leo as he moved forward. She pleaded with him without words for him to save her, but he only shook his head the slightest bit. He wasn't going to save her no matter what they did to her. But he didn't move fast enough, because Rico stepped forward and grabbed her arm, yanking her up from the bed in a painful way.

"I was getting to her," Leo said, his voice sounding strained.

"Don't get attached to another one like you did before," Rico snapped. "It won't end well for you *or* the girl."

"I'm not attached," Leo snapped. "I just have different methods from you."

"We have a job to do and we've been well instructed on how to do it. You aren't paid to think," Rico replied.

"Whatever," Leo said.

He then left the room, leaving Mary alone with Rico. The leer in the man's eyes was her only warning before he grabbed her, pressing her body up against his and smashing his mouth to hers.

Mary tried not to gag as he assaulted her mouth, but he knew how disgusted she was anyway. When he pulled back, she refused to let more tears fall, but she was barely holding it together.

"You had better get used to me, baby, cause I can either be your friend or your enemy, and let me assure you that you won't like me as the latter," he said before running his tongue across her chin.

She shuddered. Her only hope was in the words they'd spoken earlier, that they weren't allowed to do certain things to her. She hoped they feared their master enough to obey his rules.

She didn't reply to him and finally he pulled back, then grabbed her arm and began marching her toward the training room. She'd rather be anywhere other than that dungeon of hell. But Mary didn't get a choice. They didn't even want to allow her to think.

Survival for the sake of her brother was the only thing Mary had to hold on to, and she gripped that thought with intense desperation.

CHAPTER ELEVEN

MARY TOOK HALTING steps as Rico led her down the long, dark hallway. He clung tightly to her arm as he steadily moved forward, making her trip several times. There was no chance of escape — and he was telling her that with actions instead of words.

When they got into the torture room, Mary halted, and Rico tugged her more firmly, forcing her forward. They weren't alone as they'd been for the past few days. Of course Leo and Rock were there, but also Patty and another girl Mary hadn't yet met were with them.

What was happening now? Mary was completely thrown. Patty was standing in the center of the room next to the other girl, and her face was down, her eyes focused on the floor. Mary wanted to scream at her, to tell her to look up, to tell her what was going to happen next.

Rico shoved Mary next to Patty and finally let go of her arm. There were bruises where his fingers had sunk into her skin. She feared they would be the least of the welts on her body in the upcoming time she was at this horrific place.

"What is going on?" she whispered to Patty.

The girl didn't turn to look at her, didn't make a movement. "Shh," she said so quietly Mary wondered if she had imagined it.

"Strip them," Rock said, his voice sounding bored. How many times and how many girls had he done this with? Was it so routine he just didn't give a damn anymore?

Without hesitation, Rico moved over to the unknown girl and tugged her gown off, leaving her trembling as she silently cried. He then did the same to Patty before he stopped in front of Mary.

"You should always be naked," he said with a leer before stripping her gown off her.

Mary trembled with the urge to cover herself, but she knew it did no good, so instead, her hands remained at her sides as she stood there, not knowing what would come next. Each day was a new torture — each moment painful.

"Up the rations of food slightly for Mary," Rock said as he circled the three girls. "Take some away from Blaire, and leave Patty's the same."

As he circled them, his fingers ran over their bodies and Mary felt as if she were a piece of cattle being analyzed before she was sent to the slaughter. She suddenly knew this was to break them down even more. The men wanted them to know they were nothing — would never be anything. The sooner they accepted this fact, the better off they'd be.

"Patty has an open wound. Don't make it worse," Rock continued. "You know the boss doesn't appreciate that. It will come out of your hides if it continues."

The men facing them nodded. Mary glanced at Rico and he seemed disappointed by Rock's command. Mary didn't understand how any person could enjoy inflicting such misery on someone else. If she ever made it out of this situation she might actually try to figure out why that was.

"Where do you belong, Patty?" Rock asked.

Patty didn't hesitate. "With the master," she said, not looking up.

"And what will you do for him?" Rock continued.

"Whatever pleases him," she said. Her voice was devoid of emotion as if she'd said these same words a thousand times.

"Where is your home, Blaire?" he asked.

"Here," she said, her voice deader than Patty's.

"Where?" Rock said, his voice rising. Mary couldn't figure out what Blaire had said wrong.

"My home is wherever the master wants it to be," Blaire replied, her voice slightly choked.

"Was that really so hard to remember?" Rock asked before his hand shot out and he slapped the girl across her cheek, leaving a red welt. She didn't even cry or flinch at the gesture. Mary was even more horrified.

"I'm sorry," she said.

"Not good enough," Rock told her. "Rico, she needs a lesson," he continued.

Rico smiled with glee before grabbing Blaire's arm and leading her away. Mary wanted to defend the girl — wanted to stop whatever was going to happen, but how could she? Mary was just as trapped as the other two. Rico and Blaire disappeared and Mary wondered if she would ever see the girl again.

"Elena," Rock said and Mary looked around the room. There weren't any other girls.

Suddenly Rock was in front of Mary and his hand shot out, her face instantly stinging where he'd slapped her. She didn't understand.

"I called your name. I expect a reply," he told her.

"I ... I don't understand," Mary told him.

He slapped her again, this time on the other cheek. Mary couldn't keep the tears at bay, even though she desperately wanted to. She looked past Rock to where Leo was standing and pleaded with him with her eyes to help her. He looked away, but not before she saw a pained expression on his face.

"You aren't too bright, are you?" Rock said. His spit flew in her face and she fought back her gag reflex. When she did that, she really ticked these men off.

"No, sir," she replied meekly.

Rock laughed. "It's pretty simple, Elena," he said, looking into her eyes. She didn't know why he was calling her that. Then she remembered Patty's words to not forget who she was no matter what they did. This must be what her roommate had been warning her about. They were going to call her Elena. She didn't care. "You are no longer Mary. You are Elena. If you do what you're told, it won't be such a bad experience for you, it might even be pleasant. If you don't do as you're told, I guarantee you'll wish you were never born."

Mary said nothing as she didn't know what he wanted her to say. She desperately wanted to look to the ground, but she didn't do that either. She looked Rock in the eyes and waited.

"Do you understand?" he said, leaning in closer, his horrid breath invading her nostrils.

"Yes," she said simply.

"Do you want to be here, Elena?" he asked with a smirk.

She knew the wise thing would be to say yes, but she couldn't get the word from her throat. Maybe she was a fool, and maybe she had a death wish. She wasn't sure what it was, but she looked him in the eye with fury running though her.

"I would rather be anywhere else on earth," she told him.

Rock looked stunned for several heartbeats, and then an evil glint lit his eyes. She fought not to shake as he circled behind her. She had no doubt she would be punished for her insubordination. Her moment of strength wouldn't be worth it in the end. She knew that for sure.

"You are going to be fun to break," Rock whispered in her ear before his hands came up and tightened around her throat. Mary struggled against him as she lost the ability to breathe. Her vision began to go dark, but not before she saw Leo take a step toward them.

"If you take this too far, the master is going to be pissed," Leo hissed.

Rock released her and she fell to the floor, too weak to stand up.

"You don't have a right to say anything to me," Rock said.

"I'm just pointing out a fact," Leo told him, his voice just as cold as Rock's.

"Yes, my temper gets me in trouble sometimes," Rock said before he stood in front of Mary and Patty again. "Stand up, Elena," he shouted.

On shaking legs, Mary rose to her feet, trembling as she stood next to Patty who hadn't uttered a word the entire time she'd been losing her life. Mary felt even more betrayed. But then again, she hadn't said anything when Blaire had been dragged from the room.

They were all scared. The worst thing they could possibly do would be to turn on each other. Mary knew that was something she would have to remind herself of often as this torture continued.

"I think it's time for the day's lessons," Rock finally said. "Take Patty upstairs to get ready, and then come back," he told Leo.

Leo grabbed Patty and she obediently followed him. She didn't look at Mary again. Standing there naked, she waited to see what Rock was going to say next. He moved over to a couch and sat down, seeming at perfect ease.

"Come here," he told her.

Mary didn't move from where she was. She told herself to walk, but she was frozen to the floor. Rock glared at her.

"I won't repeat myself again," he told her, his fingers twitching.

Knowing she wasn't going to get away with multiple acts of defiance, Mary slowly walked to him. When she got within grabbing distance, he reached for her, making her stumble forward so she was standing between his legs, his hands on her hips.

"Sometimes I really hate the rules," he said as his fingers dug into her flesh. She felt so exposed as he kicked her legs out and examined every inch of her. "There is no doubt you're very aware of your appeal," he added, the words seeming to be more for himself than for her.

Rico's hands crawled up her body and she whimpered when he cupped her breasts. He squeezed and pain shot through her. There was nothing gentle about this man. He wanted to hurt her — to punish her — in every possible way. She tugged against him, but that only made him squeeze her that much harder. She couldn't help the yelp of pain from escaping.

When he pinched her, Mary squealed and jerked back, causing her to trip and fall to the floor. Rock looked furious as he dropped to the floor with her, his hands bracing on either side of her face, his mouth firm, his eyes deadly.

"Don't you dare try to get away from me. You will do what I want when I want. Do you understand?" he commanded, his face only an inch from hers.

He leaned back, slapped her hard enough to make her see stars, then loomed over her. Mary tried to calm the shivers racking her body, but she was going into survival mode. She didn't know how to do this, didn't know how to endure. She'd never come close to being in any situation even close to resembling this one.

Rock stood up and resumed his position on the couch. Mary stayed where she was, waiting for his next command. No matter the pain, she was going to do her best to do what she was told. It seemed to hurt a little bit less that way.

"Stand up," he told her.

Pulling herself from the ground, it took a moment for Mary to rise to her feet. Her knees were shaking so badly, she hardly heard the return of Leo. She saw him from the corner of her eye as he leaned against the wall and watched what was happening. She didn't look at him this time, fearing it would warrant more of Rock's wrath.

"Time for you to learn today's lessons," he told her. "We might not be able to do all we want with you, but I guarantee a lot of pleasure can be had anyway," he said. She in no way trusted the look in his eyes.

He reached for his pants, and Mary was horrified when he pulled himself free, scooting to the edge of the couch. Leo moved behind her and forced her down to her knees.

"If you put that anywhere near me, I will break it," Mary said. She didn't know who was more shocked — Rock, Leo or herself. They all went still, Rock's fingers clenched around himself and Leo tensed behind her.

Rock recovered the fastest, and he was smart enough to not pull her forward, but punishment was still swift. He punched her so hard, she fell to the floor, nearly passing out. Curses were shouted across the room and she curled up into a ball, wondering if she'd pushed him too far. She almost hoped so. Then this could end.

When she felt hands on her again, she screamed and flailed, feeling her fingers connect with skin. She went crazy. There was no way she was doing this. She might realize that punishment would be swift and severe, but what other choice did she have.

Another curse was rent through the air before a fist connected with her cheek. The world went dark.

CHAPTER TWELVE

"WHAT'S YOUR NAME?"

Shaking in her chair, Mary knew what they wanted to hear, but she couldn't say the name. She couldn't convincingly tell them she was Elena. They would know she was lying. They'd punish her no matter what she said because she wasn't allowed to lie to them. They always seemed to know.

She just wasn't sure which punishment would be worse.

"Did you forget how to speak?"

The deceptive words were spoken quietly, which was worse than the yelling. When they spoke quietly, it was because they were getting excited. They would get to inflict pain upon her.

She barely flinched when the whip came out and slapped against her naked thighs. There were already welts there, both old and new. She wasn't sure how much more her skin could take before it began tearing.

Patty assured her they wouldn't break the skin, but Mary wasn't convinced. The pain was unbelievable as the whip came down again, never in the same place, but still excruciating.

"What's your name?"

This time her *trainer* whispered in her ear, his hot breath slithering against her neck.

"Mary. My name is Mary," she answered with a whimper.

When the strap came down it hit her on the inner thigh, and she screamed in agony. It slammed down again, hitting her other thigh, up high where the skin was particularly sensitive. Tears rolled down her cheeks. She should be used to this. But she wasn't.

She'd been held captive for three months. For three months she hadn't spoken to her mother or her little brother, for three months she had barely been fed enough to survive, and for three months she'd been tortured nearly daily.

At the moment, she was strapped to a chair, wearing only a tight tank top and scant panties, her legs tied open to the legs of the chair, her hands tied behind the chair's back. She couldn't move, couldn't shield herself from the continuing blows.

They'd been in this session for two hours, and her body shook from the torture it had been put through. At least her day was almost over.

Earlier she'd been strapped to a chair in the other room, the room where they played videos over and over again, where they whispered the name Elena repeatedly, telling her that's who she was, that she was from Oregon, she was a runaway who had found a new home. They told her the same lies day after day.

Headphones covered her ears when they weren't whispering in them, with music blasting, her name flashing in and out while strobe lights blinded her eyes in between the videos that played, horrible movies first, then family films they said were her relatives, her mother and father. She didn't know those people — they weren't her family.

But they wanted her to believe they were. They wanted to break her. She wished she *would* break because then maybe the pain would end, maybe she wouldn't hurt all the time anymore.

Sometimes she was naked, sometimes scantily clothed. She hadn't seen Leo for over a month. Maybe he'd gotten in trouble for helping her. She didn't know, but she looked for him all the time.

If he came back she might get a reprieve. She didn't know. All she knew was she was in pain. Her body ached; her mind was mush. Wouldn't it be better to believe she was Elena? Wouldn't that make the pain go away?

Some mornings when she woke up they would ask her who she was, and she would say Elena. But then after the fog cleared, vague memories of her old life would flash through her brain, memories of her mother, of her little brother.

Often she couldn't remember what color her brother's hair was, couldn't remember what his eyes looked like. And her mother was just a blur. They were fading — just as her captors wanted them to.

However, every night she told herself she was Mary. She was born on October thirty-first, nineteen ninety-seven. She was now seventeen years old, even though she hadn't celebrated her last birthday.

But she remembered. Maybe it was time to forget. Maybe if she just forgot, the pain would stop. Patty said she wasn't beaten much anymore, that there were worse tortures than being hit, than being yelled at.

Elena — no! — Mary, shuddered as she tried not to think about what those tortures could be.

"She's done for the day. Get her out of here," Rock snapped.

"Does she eat tonight?" Rico asked.

"No. Let her think about that the next time she answers my questions."

She didn't know all of her trainers' names. She was only to call them Sir. They were cruel, loved to hold on to the whip, and loved the sound it made as it soared through the air. All of them were definitely happy with their job.

She'd yet to meet the master of the house. She wasn't complaining. That wasn't something she wanted to do — not ever, if she could help it.

One man untied her, and Mary didn't have the strength to rise. She tried, but her legs kept failing her.

"Get her out of here," Rock hollered before his bare hand smacked across her cheek, knocking her off the chair.

No tears were left. She prayed for darkness to come, but it was just past her vision, not allowing her the peace of its respite. She didn't bother opening her eyes again, nor did she try to stand. Her arms were numb from being bound too tightly for so long. She just lay in a loose mess on the floor. She couldn't care less at this point if she messed herself. She hadn't eaten or drunk anything for a day, maybe a few days, so there was nothing in her system to worry about.

"I've got this. She's done for a while."

Her ears perked up, but she still couldn't open her eyes. That was Leo. It had to be his voice. It was kinder, deeper than the other men's.

"Fine. She's your problem," the other man said before she felt the floor vibrating as he walked away.

Mary wanted to open her eyes, wanted to verify it was Leo, but she knew it was. She just wanted the reassurance of seeing one person's face who had yet to hurt her.

She felt him lift her. His rough hands slid beneath her thighs, and he carried her back to her room. He was so much gentler than the other men. She wanted to lean into him, but that wouldn't be wise. Even if he were the lesser of the evils, he was still a part of this operation. He was still the enemy.

She felt her bed meet her back, and she almost sighed as her pounding head felt the softness of the thin pillow.

"You're going to have to give something here," Leo said softly, his hand sweeping across her brow.

She opened her lips to speak, but no words would come out. Maybe her vocal cords were severed from the many times the men's hands had been around her neck.

"Rest right now. But soon, you really are going to have to give in, Elena. The torture will lessen when you just accept this is who you are now."

She felt more tears spring up behind her closed lids. She shook her head the tiniest bit. She wanted to tell him she would, but the blurred image of her brother fading away kept her from speaking.

He said nothing else. Soon, she heard the door close as Leo walked out. Shivering on top of the bed, she didn't have enough strength to pull her covers up over her.

"Mary, you need to do what he says."

The kind voice came from Patty, and Mary was grateful as her covers were pulled over her trembling body.

"I don't know how," Mary whispered weakly.

"My real name isn't Patty. My real name is Jennifer. I still remember, but I let Jennifer go a long time ago. It's dangerous for me to tell you this. But I want you to know you can still hold on to the old you, while letting the new person in," she quietly whispered.

"Why do I need a new name?" Mary asked, shivering beneath her bedding.

"Because your old self can't handle what's to come," Patty told her.

"What could they possibly do to me that hasn't already been done?" Mary cried.

"I don't think you want the answer to that," Patty said with a sniffle.

"I'm Mary, I'm Mary," she quietly whispered several times.

Her old life was fading away, and she was so afraid that if it completely vanished, she would never be able to go back. She would never keep her promise to her little brother.

"I'm going to start calling you Elena now. Don't be upset with me. But I think it's time you begin to believe you're Elena because if you don't they will kill you. I've never seen a girl take as much abuse as you've taken," she began, "and live through it."

Mary was ready to die. Each new day she lost hope that she would ever see her family again, so what was the point of continuing on? If this was what was in store for her for the rest of her life, she'd rather die.

"Elena, I'm going to help you sit up," Patty said as she sat on the edge of the bed and placed an arm beneath her.

"Just want to sleep," she mumbled.

"I snuck in a snack for you," Patty told her.

Patty pulled her up and then Elena — Mary — Elena, heck, she didn't know, felt something cool against her lips. She tried to suck, but she didn't even have the energy for that. Slowly the liquid dripped down her throat. Just that small amount of coolness gave her enough energy to open her eyes.

"There you go. Have a little more, and then I'll give you a piece of bread, but you can't say anything or we'll both be punished," Patty whispered.

"Won't tell," Mary mumbled.

Maybe it was better not to have it, but she couldn't turn it down, not when Patty put it to her lips. It was a small roll, and she nibbled on it. After the first two tiny bites, she was able to hold it. She wanted to stuff it all into her mouth, but she also wanted it to last.

Patty moved to her bed and sat down as Mary slowly ate the bread.

"Thank you, Patty," she told her friend.

"You have to start thinking of yourself as Elena," Patty repeated.

"It's already getting so foggy," Mary told her, panic once again setting in.

"Your life will get so much easier if you just let go," Patty said, her voice sad.

"Did you let go?" she challenged.

"Yes. I let go of my old life. No, I haven't completely forgotten it, but I let it go. Then I wasn't so sad all the time. Yes, I still hurt, and yes, some days are worse than others, but the pain you're going through right now eventually stopped for me. I shouldn't have told you to remember. I'm sorry, Elena."

"I don't want to forget," Mary said.

"You just need to push it aside. Then, if you ever get the chance, it will all come back to you," Patty promised.

Mary lay there that night in bed, and instead of repeating her name and birthday, she fell asleep telling herself over and over again, *I'm Elena.*

It was time for Elena to become real — and for Mary to die. She just didn't know how to make that happen.

CHAPTER THIRTEEN

THE SCREEN FLASHED, the images making Mary's stomach dip into her legs. She'd seen these images a hundred times, maybe a thousand. She didn't know why, but they still made her sick.

This was her life — or what her life would soon be. How she wished they would just kill her. They threatened it enough. Why wouldn't they just come out and end her life? She was trying to cooperate with them, but it still wasn't enough.

And if the images on the screen were a clear indication of what was to come, she wanted nothing to do with it. She hadn't even kissed a boy before being at this house, let alone done the things that were on that screen.

The next video began.

A man held a woman tied to a bed while a whip flung through the air, hitting her until her body, from her neck to her ankles, was red and swollen. The woman had a hood over her head, but with each hit of the whip, a soft cry escaped.

How she wasn't bleeding, Mary didn't know. When the man was finished, he moved to the head of the bed and ripped off the hood. To Mary's horror, the person on the bed was Patty. She smiled at the man, and Mary knew the girl enough to know it wasn't a real smile. It was the one she had shown Mary she used to make the master happy.

"Did you enjoy that, Patty?" he asked as his hand ran down her body. The touch had to hurt with her reddened skin.

"Yes, Master," Patty said, a soft purr to her voice.

"Do you want more?" he asked, excitement clear in his tone.

"If that's what pleases you, Master," Patty said.

Mary could see the tenseness in Patty's body, but the master didn't see it, or just didn't care. This was Mary's first image of the man they'd been grooming her for all these months.

The sight of him as he crawled up on the bed and began fondling Patty made her want to vomit. He was old, with wrinkling skin, a saggy belly, and thinning white hair. She couldn't see his eyes in the video, but as he sank himself into Patty and began thrusting inside the tied-up girl, rolls of fat on his back and ass shook while he grunted and moaned. When he was finished he stood up and stared down triumphantly at the young girl on his bed, a smirk on his face.

"I'm growing bored with you," he said.

"I apologize, Master. What can I do to make you happier?" she asked, her body showing a slight tremble.

"Our time might be up," he replied before walking away.

Mary watched her friend. She showed no reaction to this. She simply lay there. A few of the men who'd tortured her day in and day out came up to the bed and untied the girl.

The master walked back into the room with a robe now tied around him.

"You can do what you want with her. I want to meet the new girl," he said.

The men looked at Patty as she rubbed her sore wrists, sitting on the bed, not trying to move away.

"Thank you, Sir. We'll enjoy her," one of the men said before roughly yanking Patty to her feet.

"Your graciousness is most generous," the other man said before grabbing Patty's other arm.

"Enjoy," the master said.

The screen went dark.

Mary sat in the chair shivering. Why had they shown her this particular video? They'd shown plenty of videos of people having sex, but never one of the master and Patty. Were they showing the future of her own life, or were they telling her she had better be ready?

"Did you enjoy the show?"

Mary gulped as the men walked into the room, joining her. She said nothing. Mary wasn't sure what they wanted her to say.

"The master is ready for you. You'd best be ready for him."

The men laughed as they untied her and roughly pushed her to her feet. "Let's get you cleaned up."

No matter how hard she tried, Mary couldn't stop trembling. This was the end of the line for her. There really wasn't going to be an escape.

CHAPTER FOURTEEN

DAYS PASSED AND Mary was told she was Elena so often, she began referring to herself by that name. It was easier. She was beginning to feel like Elena. Mary was weak and pathetic, but Elena was strong, able to withstand torture. *Elena* didn't cry for home, didn't miss her little brother. Elena knew she was nothing more than a tool to make a man happy. Elena didn't need to worry about messy emotions.

But Mary kept trying to seep through, kept trying to remind Elena that she was still inside of her. Elena pushed her farther away. Mary was too emotional, too clingy. She had to go away.

When her door began to open, she sat up, hands on her knees, back straight. That's how they wanted her to wait. They wanted her to be obedient. If she was obedient they didn't start her day by slapping her face.

Yes, she'd still get hit, they enjoyed hitting her, but the torture seemed to come down a notch when they were pleased with her.

She could make them happy. She would do whatever it took to please them.

When Leo filled her doorway, she smiled the slightest bit. He was beginning to come around more often again. The torture was never quite as bad with Leo. Yes, he also took a turn on the whip once in a while, but there was no joy in his eyes and the lashes didn't go on as long.

He'd told her once he was just doing his job. Maybe he was. She forgave him for hurting her, because he always was gentle afterward, and always said kind words to her before leaving her to recover in her little room.

"How are you feeling today, Elena?" he asked as he moved in front of her.

"I'm feeling better than yesterday," she told him.

"That's good," he said. "You get a little break today. We want to clean you up."

Elena still hated the showers. The men were pretty much allowed to do anything they wanted to her, and they took full advantage of that fact. There was nothing sacred about her body. They hadn't forced sex on her but had pushed her to the point where she would lie in a fetal position rocking after they were finished releasing their seed all over her.

Why in the world would anyone anticipate sex? From what she'd discovered in the past few months, it was dirty, violent, and all about the man. She couldn't imagine the act being erotic or pleasurable for a woman. How were children still brought into the world?

Still, when Leo held out his hand, she obediently stood and followed him. He'd beckoned her, so she had no other choice but to go and do whatever this new day would bring her.

She was almost ready to give up on escaping. It was much easier on her mind to simply become Elena. Why not? Letting go of the past was the only thing allowing her to move forward, accept what was in front of her.

Leo bathed her, the experience much less traumatic than the other men doing it, but still a violation against her body. Of course, it wasn't hers anymore, was it? No. It belonged to the master of the house and the men there to train her.

She must remember that. When Leo finished, she stood still while he dressed her in scanty clothing, and then she followed him to the chair. No one else was in the room.

"Do you still want to be saved, Elena?" he asked while tying her legs down.

What was she supposed to say to that? Of course she wanted to be saved.

"You can be honest with me," he said as he looked around. "No one is listening right now." His eyes told her they could be trusted, but everything in her experience so far told her no one could be trusted. She'd asked this very thing from Leo before and he'd refused her. So was this a test? She just didn't know anymore.

"There's no one to save me," she finally said. "This is now my fate." She didn't tell him she often dreamt of running away, of finding her way home.

"I could save you," he said as he stood and cupped her cheek.

Her heart accelerated at his words. Had he decided to be her savior? She was too emotional to say a word.

"I might just do that," he told her before securing her to the chair, her arms behind her back. He leaned forward, his breath resting on her neck. "Not now. But soon I could save you."

With that promise in the air, the door opened and Leo stood, his face once again a mask as he backed up and waited. The other men joined them as they examined her.

"Good job, Leo," one of the men said.

"Let's play a movie. The boss might not make it down after all," another told them.

Strobe lights were turned low and the screen flashed with images of the family they kept telling her was hers.

When the end of the day came and went she was dragged back to her room. She let out a relieved breath. The master hadn't come. Maybe he didn't want her.

That night, she felt hope for the first time in a while. Maybe Leo really was going to be her savior. Or maybe he would take her farther into the pits of hell. She just didn't know anymore.

CHAPTER FIFTEEN

"SHE'S NOT QUITE broken yet, Sir. I don't know if it's safe for you to be down here."

"Don't tell me where I can and cannot be in my own house. Move aside."

Strapped to a chair, her ties the only thing holding her up, Elena watched as a large man with silver hair circled her chair, examining her. She recognized him immediately but tried to push it from her brain. He was the man on the video, the man with the cruel smile and harsh hand.

"Why isn't she broken?" the master asked, his fingers on his chin as he analyzed her. Elena looked back down. She couldn't muster the energy for disgust right now.

"She's strong. Much stronger than any of the girls we've dealt with before, Sir."

"Hmm." He continued circling her. "She's scrawny and looks like shit." The man inspected her like she was nothing more than one of a herd of cattle ready for the slaughter, and he was determining how much he could get per pound. Maybe that's exactly what she was.

Elena could barely maintain her grasp on reality. She wasn't sure who or what she was anymore. There was a vague echo in the back of her mind, that she wasn't Elena, that she'd once been someone else, been someone happy and carefree.

But the more days that had passed, the more that echo died, and the more she felt she was dying. She might be nothing more than an empty shell. She really didn't know.

"We've limited her food during her conversion. Most women would have broken by now."

"Maybe it's time we give up on this one," he said, no emotion in his tone. He continued staring at her. Though she was no longer looking at the man, she could feel his gaze burning into her.

"I would normally tell you, yes, we should. But in this case, she's almost there. It's been time-consuming, but I think the harder they fall, the more broken they are. I wouldn't stop now. Too much has been invested," her trainer said.

"That's good to hear. I like the look of this one." The silver-haired man moved forward and suddenly clasped her chin tightly in his grasp. "Yes, I really like the look of this one," he murmured.

Disgust — as much as she was able to feel at this point in her life — filled Elena at the old man's touch. There was nothing she could do about it though. Even if she hadn't been tied down, she was too weak to fight him — to fight anyone.

He trailed his slimy fingers down her shirtless body and then forcibly pinched her nipples. She was used to the abuse, and she didn't give him the satisfaction of crying out. He pulled back and grinned. She looked at his nose, refusing to make eye contact with the monster.

"Yes, I really like this one. Keep working on her." When she thought it was over, the man turned to her trainer and smiled. "I want a few minutes alone."

"Sir, she's secure right now, but she still fights us once in a while," the trainer warned.

"Check her restraints, then leave us," he thundered, obviously not liking it when he was argued with.

Her trainer did as his boss demanded, and the four goons walked from the room, the click of the door signaling she was now alone with the master.

"You are a fighter, aren't you, Elena?" he asked as his hand rested on her upper thigh. It took so much effort for her not to flinch.

"I'm sorry, Sir," she said when she knew he was expecting an answer from her.

He squeezed her thigh hard, nearly making her cry out. She barely managed to hold it back.

"I would take you right now, but I want to savor this," he said with a smile. "Though, it has been a couple weeks for me."

His expression was conflicted as he reached up and clasped one breast, squeezing it as hard as her thigh. This time he managed to get a small squeak from her.

"No. I will wait . . ." he said with a pause. "But not too much longer. If you aren't broken soon, then I'll be the one to break you."

His eyes glowed at that statement as if this was a new concept that greatly excited him. He was such a monster. How could anyone work for him?

He knelt in front of her, his face level with hers, and then he was gripping the back of her neck, bracing her as he moved to her lips. She didn't fight the kiss. What good would it do? But her stomach turned as his tongue thrust into her mouth and his other hand moved down her body, touching her breasts, pulling the nipples roughly, before sliding down her stomach and penetrating her sore opening.

When he pulled back, his eyes glowed with excitement. "It's so difficult to wait," he murmured as if he were changing his mind. She knew this was going to happen, but she wasn't ready. They hadn't emptied her mind enough for her to survive it.

He leaned down and bit her nipple, making another whimper escape from her as she heard the zipper of his pants go down. She fought the tears wanting to escape. She had no doubt that would excite him even more.

He didn't bother looking at her face but continued assaulting her breasts as she heard the slapping sound of him pleasuring himself. She tried taking herself to another place, any place but where she was, but she couldn't escape the sound of him grunting as one hand punctured her body while his other pleasured himself.

When he released her throbbing nipple and let out a cry, she felt moist fluid against her leg. She had to fight against gagging.

"Yes, I won't wait much longer. The idea of taming you overrides my men's fear of you somehow being able to escape or hurt me," he said with a laugh. Of course he didn't think it possible for her to hurt him. She wasn't capable of hurting anyone in her weak condition.

He stood, his waning erection still hanging out. He rubbed the tip against her lips and laughed again before moving back and tucking himself into his pants.

"I'll return soon," he promised.

The master left the room. She fought tears, refusing to let them fall. It wasn't long before someone entered and dimmed the lights. Then the videos began to play before her, and Elena watched. She had no choice but to watch. She'd seen these scenes a thousand times over.

After a while, she was almost hypnotized. She felt Mary slip farther away. She pushed Mary away because Mary couldn't handle what was happening to her. Elena could. Mary was the only thing holding her back.

"Dad," she whispered as she watched the screen.

Her father was running in this video, a big smile on his face.

"Come on, Elena, you can catch me," he called, turning around and gazing at her as a child on the screen.

"I'm coming, Dad," she muttered aloud at the same time her younger version said it.

Their golden retriever chased after them, and then she caught up to her father and tackled him. He acted like she was strong, and he fell to the ground, both of them laughing as the puppy licked their faces.

"I love you, Elena," her father said between fits of laughter.

"I love you too, Daddy," she sighed before laying her head against his chest.

Then the puppy snuggled up to them, and they gazed at the sky as it began to darken and stars appeared.

The videos continued. One after the other.

Eventually, Elena fell asleep in her chair, used to passing out from malnutrition, exhaustion, or just because her body was completely worn out.

At some point, the men must have moved her as they always did, because she woke up in her bed. Bathed. Always bathed, unless she had done something wrong or something that prevented bathing. It had to be extreme on her part because the animals liked her clean, liked to smell her as they laid their filthy hands all over her.

"I'm Elena. I'm seventeen years old. My parents died. I ran away and got sick." This was what she was supposed to say every day. She had to say it over and over again. Over and over and over and . . .

Elena fell back asleep.

In her dream, a blond little boy ran up to her, his arms open wide, but she couldn't see his face. Couldn't hear what he was saying to her. But watching him run to her made her smile. He was so precious, this little boy with no name. There was such light radiating from him. She wanted to know him.

She knew she wasn't allowed to know this boy. She didn't know why, but she knew.

"I'm Elena. I'm seventeen years old. My parents died . . .

CHAPTER SIXTEEN

THE DOOR HADN'T latched. Elena lay in her bed, shallow breaths coming in and out. The door wasn't locked. She did nothing. Seconds ticked by, and then minutes, maybe even an hour and she still lay in her bed.

Was this a test?

She wasn't sure. But it could be that one of her captors had been in a hurry, had wanted to get to the ball game he'd been talking about with the other guys. Maybe she could escape. The thought hadn't crossed her mind in a long while. That was a thought from Mary, never something Elena would even sort of think about.

But the door hadn't latched.

Terror seizing her throat shut, her heart thudding a million miles a minute, Elena stood very quietly. If they were somehow on the other side of the door, she would regret ever turning that knob.

But if they weren't — if she truly were alone — she might be able to escape; she just might make it out to a place where no one hit her, no one touched her, where she could figure out who she truly was.

Elena wasn't sure anymore. She wasn't sure of anything.

Taking tiny steps, it took her at least fifteen minutes to go the short distance from her bed to the door. She stopped with each step and listened, trying to hear the sound of breathing, of whispering, of anything out of place.

When nothing registered, she lifted her hand to the doorknob and placed her fingers there. Tears sprung to her eyes; she was so scared. Her hand shook, and she had to reach out and hold it with her other hand to keep it from rattling the doorknob.

Elena had no idea how much time passed with her standing just like that, unwilling to make that little turn that would tell her if she could get away or not.

Finally, maybe after an hour, maybe only five minutes, she began turning the knob. It didn't resist the motion. When it was all the way turned, she was shocked and delighted to feel the weight of the door give. All she had to do was pull it inward and then there would be an opening for her to escape.

Inch by terrifying inch, she managed to open the door enough to poke her head out and look up and down the hallway. She'd only been led to the right to where the bathroom, theatre room, and torture chamber were. She'd never been to the left. That had to be the way to freedom.

Stepping into the hallway, she carefully closed the door behind her and looked down the hallway for long minutes. She couldn't keep her body from shaking and didn't try to stop it as she began creeping to the left.

The corridor seemed endless, but eventually she made it around a bend, and then right before her was a set of stairs. The hallway was dim; shadows were cast everywhere from low wattage lights that hung sporadically from the ceiling.

When she reached the stairs she saw another door at the top. Okay, she could handle that. Maybe it was locked and this journey would be over. Maybe there was someone on the other side, and her escape would be thwarted. But maybe no one would be there, and she could free herself of this hell.

Elena tested each step before putting any weight on it. She kept to the edges. Some distant memory told her that the closer to the wall she stepped the less likely there would be a chance of squeaking if the boards were loose.

Climbing the stairs took her nearly as long as it had taken her to cross her small room, but finally she reached the top. She stood next to the door with her ear pressed against it as she listened for sounds. Was there someone on the other side? She didn't hear a thing, and no light was shining beneath it. Elena truly might be alone.

Lifting her hand, she touched the gold doorknob and centimeter by centimeter she began to turn it. It kept on twisting. When it was all the way to the left, she began pushing the door, hoping it wouldn't make a sound.

Her luck continued. The door opened and no light came into the stairwell as she opened it wider. After a while there was a big enough area for her to poke her head through. The room in front of her was dark, but she saw something that gave her hope.

Windows that had light coming in through them.

She pushed the door a little more and then slipped through it, carefully shutting it without a sound behind her. She then leaned on the wall and looked around the small room.

She had no idea where she was, but it was rustic with a lawn mower over in the corner and a workbench against one wall. It appeared as if she were in a finished shed, or a barn, possibly a work building. Maybe this place wasn't attached to the main house. That would be good. She wouldn't risk passing someone if she was somewhere away from the house.

She stayed along the wall as she crept quickly inside the shed until she found another door, a small gap at the bottom letting in air, telling her this had to lead to the outside. Joy filled her heart.

She quickly lifted her arm and set her hand on the doorknob before she stopped herself. This wasn't the time to get careless. She needed to remain alert. Taking her hand away, she listened to see if she could hear anything.

There wasn't a sound. Still, she waited another ten minutes or so before she raised her hand back to the doorknob. When she tried to turn this knob, though, her stomach tensed. It was locked. She put more pressure on it, but it wasn't budging.

She nearly whimpered in her disappointment. She was so close to freedom or felt like she was. Before giving up, though, Elena looked around the room, her eyes coming to a large window across from her.

Keeping her back pressed against the wall, she moved over to the curtainless window and again listened for any sound. Her patience was waning as the need for freedom called to her.

She heard nothing, crawled under the window, slowly lifted her head, and peeked out. The yard was dark, and she scanned the area for a long time, not seeing anyone patrolling the grounds.

Elena rose and found a latch on the window, which she easily undid. Maybe the lock on the door she hadn't been able to open was to keep people out. It wasn't intended to keep someone in. Still she didn't let out a full breath until the window slid up easily.

She was done being slow now. If she was going to get caught, she wasn't going to make it easy for the men who had been torturing her month after month. She lifted the window enough to squeeze through and then hefted her body up and over the sill, quickly falling to the other side.

The crunch of the ground below her made too loud a sound, and she shrank back as she listened for approaching steps. When none came her way, Elena stood and quickly shut the window, not wanting someone to spot it and know she'd escaped. Maybe an extra three minutes would be the difference between freedom and escape.

She decided she couldn't move too fast, but she couldn't crawl either. Elena stepped away from the wall and began to run toward the darkest part of the yard, away from the shed. The other way must be the house, because a house would definitely have light on it.

She ran and ran, not knowing how far she was getting or if the yard would ever end. Maybe there wasn't a fence. Maybe she was already off the property. Joy filled her. But as she continued to move, she did see a fence up ahead in the dim moonlight.

And then she heard the dogs. No! She was so close to freedom.

Elena picked up her pace, her eyes focused on the fence ahead of her. It was a tall brick wall. She didn't care. She would scale it. Her breath rushing from her lungs, she reached the wall and jumped up, trying to get a foothold. She fell down and looked up and down the fence, searching for a place she could crawl over. If she could just get over the fence she would be free. There had to be neighbors, cars driving by.

Just as she had that thought, she heard the sweet sound of a motor as a vehicle passed by. She screamed, no longer caring to be quiet. They were coming for her. She practically felt their hot breath on her neck.

The car kept going, but Elena screamed again as she tried to mount the fence. Even when her hair was yanked back and a hand slammed over her mouth, she still tried to scream and claw herself forward.

Escape was so close. If she could just get over the fence.

"Where do you think you're going?" one of her captors asked. "I step out for a few minutes and you try to make a run for it. Your punishment will be quite fun for me," he finished as he began dragging her backward.

She fought against him; even when his fist slammed into her ribs, she still kicked and bit at his hand. She'd been so close . . . so very close.

Denial hung heavy in her heart as she was pushed back into the barn.

"Let me go!" she screamed.

The man only smiled.

And Elena felt herself lose it.

CHAPTER SEVENTEEN

THE MAN DRAGGED her kicking and screaming back to her prison as his friends joined him. Though she struggled, she was no match for these men. They easily carried her down the basement stairs and threw her to the floor in the torture room.

Elena jumped from the floor and reached out, sweeping her short fingernails across the face of the man in front of her, rejoicing when she saw angry red welts instantly appear.

She knew the punishment would be a hundred times worse than what she'd just dished out, but she no longer cared. She wanted to enrage this man so badly he would kill her. Then this torture would be over.

She forced a laugh from her throat, a laugh she didn't feel.

"Did you enjoy that?" she screamed at the man and continued laughing.

The laughter morphed though, making her sound like a maniac. Maybe she was. Elena had no idea who she was anymore.

She didn't even care.

She'd tried to end her own life a couple of times, and she was always stopped. So the only way out of this situation was to enrage these men to the point that they would end her misery.

"You little bitch!" the man screamed. "You will pay for that."

She heard the sound of his fist rushing through the air, and instead of backing away from it, she leaned into the punch, his fist connecting with the side of her head, making her vision blur as she stumbled backward and fell hard on her butt.

Once on the ground, the man's shoe whipped out and her breath rushed from her body when he connected with her stomach before stepping on her hand, the sound of fingers cracking echoing off the walls. Vomit flew from her lips at the impact.

"Now who's laughing?" the man snarled as he reached down and tightened his fingers in her hair, yanking hard until she had no choice but to stand.

She was brought to her feet, facing the man. The dizziness was passing, although she was still having a hard time catching her breath. She glared at the man through her already swelling eye and then reached back in her throat before spitting in his face.

Rage, unlike anything she'd ever witnessed, flashed across his eyes as he yanked even harder on her hair, then let go only to thrust his hands out, sending her flying backward.

Her neck jerked as she hit the wall and slid down. Her head was spinning. It wouldn't take a whole lot more until she couldn't stand up. She didn't care. This was what she wanted. What she had prayed for.

Blood dripped from somewhere on her scalp, and her eye was almost completely swollen shut. Elena still managed to smirk at the man as she called him an asshole. She didn't even feel the pain of her injuries. Her adrenaline was running too high for her to feel much of anything.

Rock took a menacing step toward her when two of the other men grabbed both his arms and held him back.

"Let me go. This bitch is going to regret the day she ever met me," he snarled.

"I already do," she snapped, not breaking eye contact with the hulk.

He lunged against his friends, trying to get to her.

"This is what she wants," one man said, obviously the smartest of the four men.

"Don't give into this. The master will kill you if you permanently damage her," the other guy said.

"I don't care. I'm done with this bitch. It's been months. She's not trainable," Rock thundered.

"Everyone is trainable. She's breaking," the fourth man said as he stepped in the room with them.

"Not this one. She's too strong-willed. I've never seen any woman take this much abuse," Rock said, but he was calmer.

Elena couldn't have that. She was so close to her goal. Her head was pounding and her vision continued to blur, but she needed another push. She needed him to literally beat the life out of her.

"I think you do this because you have a small dick and want to prove your masculinity to the world," she said before spitting in his direction again as she stumbled to her feet.

His eyes glazed over and, before the other men could stop him, he was on her. He grabbed her head and slammed it backward against the wall.

The darkness that had been edging around her eyes completely filled her vision. As the lights dimmed, she could see the light-haired little boy from her dreams running toward her. She reached out to him, wanting to call his name, but having no idea who he was. She just knew she had to be with him. She rushed forward, not understanding why he never got closer. She panicked as she continued to move forward, and finally the gap closed.

Mary was the one who grabbed hold of him tightly and vowed to never let him go. She was home. This was home. She promised to never leave again.

CHAPTER EIGHTEEN

A LIGHT WAS SHINING beneath her closed eyelids, but she didn't want to open them. She had no idea why she didn't want to open them; she just knew she was safer with them closed. Fogginess rolled through her mind as she tried to figure out where she was.

But then her eyes flew open, and she looked around the fetid room. Her location wasn't the worst of the situation. No, that wasn't what scared her to her very center. What made her terrified to open her eyes was the fact that she had no idea who she was. A man sat next to her bed, looking down at a magazine. When she stirred on the mattress he looked up.

"How are you feeling, Elena?"

"What? What did you say?" she gasped, her voice quiet and scratchy.

"I asked how you're feeling?" he repeated as he leaned forward.

"Where am I?" she asked, looking around blankly.

"What do you remember?" the man asked.

She closed her eyes for a moment, but had no memories. There was a blank where she knew information should be.

"I . . . I don't know," she gasped as fear rose in her throat.

"What's your name?" he asked.

She felt tears pop into her eyes. "I . . . I don't know," she repeated.

"It's okay, darling, it's okay," he said as he laid his hand on hers.

She turned her palm and gripped his fingers. For some reason, she wanted to cling to this man she didn't remember.

"Who are you?" she asked. Maybe if he told her, something would come to her.

"I'm Leo. I'm the one who found you," he told her with a kind smile.

"Where was I?" she asked.

"You were hurt, Elena, badly hurt," he said with a shake of his head.

"From what?" She again looked around but nothing was coming to her.

"You ran away from home a long time ago and moved here, and then got upset one day and ran off. People attacked you, and you've been in a coma for several days," he explained.

"Who attacked me? Where's home?" she gasped.

"This is home, Elena, and we don't know who attacked you," he said as he lifted a calming hand and laid it against her hair.

The gesture both reassured and scared her at the same time. There was no reason for her not to believe this man.

"I'm Elena?" she asked.

"Yes. We saved you," he said.

She felt groggy as she tried to listen to what he was saying. But nothing made sense. Her world felt as if it were spinning out of control.

"I'm Elena," she quietly muttered as her lids dropped.

"Get some rest, darling. I will help you remember who you are when you're better," he told her as he gripped her fingers.

Elena closed her eyes. Yes, she just needed more rest. She was safe.

Closing her eyes, she drifted back into the darkness. Just before sleep overtook her, a bright light seemed to take away the shadows as a little boy ran away from her. She reached out, trying to catch him, but he was gone before she took her first step.

The light faded, and Elena drifted into darkness.

CHAPTER NINETEEN
One Month Later

"ELENA, ARE YOU ready?"

Turning, Elena looked at Leo, and gave him a semblance of a smile.

"Yes, I'm ready." Giving her hair another quick swoop, she set the brush down and walked from the room.

"You should make the master very happy."

She didn't even flinch at his words. After all, it was what she was supposed to do, wasn't it? Make the master happy. She didn't know why, but her entire purpose was to please the master.

Whenever her name was spoken, she felt a slight twinge inside of her, something that told her there was something wrong, but she couldn't quite figure out what that was. Why would there be a twinge?

"Come with me."

"Yes, of course, Leo."

Elena followed Leo from the bathroom, a slight limp in her left leg. She couldn't remember how she'd hurt herself. She didn't remember much. Leo told her it was because she had something called amnesia. He was her friend so why would he lie?

He walked her to a part of the house she'd never been to before, and she looked around in awe. A large, beautiful staircase twirled upward looking like it was going to the sky, and far above her she could see a balcony.

"This is a very beautiful room," she told him.

"Yes, it is." Leo didn't talk a heck of a lot. That was okay. Elena wasn't sure if she ever talked much.

She was alone a lot. There had been a girl in her room for a while, she was pretty sure. But one day she'd come back to that room, and she'd been gone. Now, Elena wasn't sure the girl had ever been there.

If only she could remember. Leo assured her that her memory would come back. That's why she watched videos. There were so many videos. Some of them triggered something in her brain, but she wasn't sure if it was because she'd seen the video before or because it was a memory. Whatever it was, they were happy thoughts, she assured herself.

"Have a seat over there. The master will be with you shortly."

Elena sat down, her legs together and to the side as Leo had taught her. She hadn't seen the other man, the man who she could only address as Master, in a long time. For some reason, that was a bad memory, but once in a while, she would wake up in a cold sweat because his face would flash across her memories.

That man had to have been from her past — the time before Leo had saved her.

Footsteps echoed in the hallway, and Elena sat up a bit higher. She had to be presentable when the master entered the room. It was her whole reason for being, after all.

"Very nice." The voice made her jump a little when he spoke.

There was a vague memory trying to scratch the surface of her brain as the silver-haired man approached with a smile that made her feel slightly uncomfortable, though she didn't understand why.

She was here for him. She was alive because of him, she told herself.

"Hello, Elena," he said as he sat down beside her

"Hi. How are you?" she replied.

"I'm much better now that I'm with you," he said as he reached over and placed his hand above her knee.

Elena felt herself wanting to pull away, but she didn't know why. He rubbed his fingers against her leg, and she closed them a little tighter. His expression instantly changed.

"Don't do that," he snarled, his grin gone.

"I'm sorry, Master," she replied, forcing her muscles to relax.

"That's better, dear," he told her, his grin coming back into place as his fingers rubbed up and down her leg.

For some reason she felt like crying. That was nonsense, she tried to assure herself.

"I want to make you happy," she told him.

"I love to hear that, darling," he said, tugging on one leg, opening them more.

She looked over at Leo who was sitting across from them. She'd been naked around him many times, but for some reason she was uncomfortable with Leo sitting across from her as the master opened her legs, exposing her panties beneath her dress.

"Are you uncomfortable?" the master asked.

"No, Master," she quickly replied. That was the answer he would want to hear.

"Good. Don't fight me," he said as his fingers trailed higher.

When he brushed the outside of her panties, she felt sick to her stomach. This wasn't right. But she didn't understand why she was feeling that it wasn't. Everything that was instilled in her was to be perfect for this man now touching her. So why wouldn't she relish attention from him.

"Come here," he said, removing his hand. She wanted to breathe out a sigh of relief until she processed his words.

"I don't understand what you'd like me to do," she told him, looking him in the eyes. There was something off about his eyes.

"I want you to stand up and sit on my lap," he told her.

She gulped, but immediately stood. "How would you like me to sit?" she asked while standing directly in front of him.

He grabbed her, knocking her off balance, and then placed her legs on either side of his so she was straddling his lap.

"Mmm, just like this," he told her as his hands wrapped around her back, and he pulled her close to him. "You smell divine."

He buried his face in her neck, and she felt the sharp pinch of his teeth when he bit her skin. It took everything inside her not to struggle against him.

Gripping her hair, he tugged her head back, his mouth now close to hers. His breath smelled of tobacco and alcohol, and she fought not to gag. This wasn't how she was supposed to feel.

He leaned in and then his cold, hard lips were pressed against hers. Elena told herself to enjoy the kiss, told herself this was right, but she was having to concentrate fully on not tensing up, on not gagging as his tongue slithered into her mouth.

When he pushed against her, she felt something hard pressing against her panties, and his eyes were gleaming with delight.

"I'm really going to enjoy this one," he said, pushing her off his lap. "She has been well worth the wait. Great job, Leo." He paused. "It's too bad I have a business meeting in town right now."

He stood up, and Elena didn't budge. She was afraid her knees would shake if she moved so much as an inch.

"Prepare her for me. Have her in my room when I get back. You know what I want," the master said to Leo.

"Yes, Sir."

Elena knew she must be wrong, but there appeared to be sympathy in Leo's eyes. That wasn't possible. He'd told her himself that she would be prepared for the master.

The silver-haired man left the room, and Elena still didn't budge. She had the distinct urge to bolt, to go running from the house and hide. But where would she go? She had nowhere to go. This was her home.

"You have an hour if you'd like to walk the grounds," Leo said.

"What's the matter, Leo?" she asked.

He shook his head. "It's nothing, Elena."

She wouldn't argue with him, but clearly something was wrong. It was too bad she couldn't figure out what that was.

"I would love to walk the grounds," she finally said.

She took a small step to make sure her knees would work. They were slightly shaky, but not so bad that she wouldn't be able to use them.

Leo stayed where he sat as she passed back the way she'd come and went out the back entrance to the small yard where she was allowed to walk.

Holding her face up, she let the sunshine beam down on her, and her stress evaporated. She couldn't remember much of anything these days, but she had a feeling it had been a long time since she'd been in the sun, more than a few weeks ago. Could she even remember the light touching her face for the first time?

Elena was always disappointed when she was called back inside, especially when she had to go to her small room where she was alone.

They didn't lock her door. She was free to get up and use the restroom or go to the sitting area and watch the many videos they had of her and her family. Those videos always made her smile.

She'd asked Leo about the locks on her door, and he'd explained that after they found her, she'd been violent, had hurt herself so they'd had to protect her. Leo was very kind.

Elena sat down and closed her eyes. Leo had told her that her life would change this night. Was she ready for that? Elena should be ready. But she wasn't so sure.

CHAPTER TWENTY

"IT'S TIME TO get ready, Elena."

Slowly opening her eyes, Elena again had the urge to run. Maybe she should have done that already. But no. Everything in her rebelled at the thought.

As she followed Leo into the house, a memory flooded through her that sent fear down to her toes. She had run once. Was it here? The fog was too great for her to know that for sure. But she'd found an opening, and she'd tried to escape. The people who had caught her had made her regret doing that. She wouldn't run away again — never!

The pain. She could almost feel the pain that had been wrought upon her. It had been so intense. She wiggled her fingers as she continued walking behind Leo. Her fingers had been broken. Her ribs cracked. Her eyes swollen shut.

No. Running away wasn't the answer.

They stepped into a large bathroom and Elena faced Leo. "I can bathe myself," she told him.

"I'm sorry, Elena, but the master's instructions are very explicit. I'm to get you ready," he told her.

This wasn't unusual. She rarely got the opportunity to bathe herself. When she did, she would stand beneath the spray, sometimes for so long that it would be freezing when she finally rinsed the soap from her hair.

But it was worth it. The water washed everything dirty away, and there was so much filth on her. She always felt unclean, felt as if she couldn't get spotless enough. So many people looked at her, touched her. A shudder rushed through her.

She stripped off her clothes, and then waited as Leo adjusted the water. Then she stepped into the tub and sat as his hands scrubbed every inch of her flesh so hard that she was red from her neck to her toes. The redness would go away. Eventually.

She didn't even mind the painful scrubbings. It really was the only time she felt somewhat clean. The antiseptic he put on next always stung. She had to close her eyes and try desperately to keep from trembling. She counted sheep in her head while Leo finished, putting a gritty stripping soap in her hair and then rinsing it all out.

"Okay, you can rinse in the shower, then dry off and meet me in the sitting room," Leo told her before he walked out.

Elena took her time rinsing off, and then slowly, carefully, towel-dried her body before looking in the mirror at her puffy skin. It was all part of the process, she assured herself.

The towel was wrapped around her when she entered the sitting room. Leo was there at the table, the cream sitting beside him. This part wasn't the worst, except for having his hands on every inch of her skin. He didn't make her afraid though.

She took her position and then let the towel drop.

"You're redder than normal," he murmured. "I'm sorry."

"It doesn't hurt," she told him.

"What in the hell is taking so long?"

Instantly Elena's body froze. That voice! It hadn't been a nightmare. What was that man doing there?

Turning to be sure it was who she thought — the face that haunted her — she began shivering when he stepped into the room. It was definitely him. Flashes of a whip flying at her rushed across her memories, and she cowered behind Leo.

"I thought you were going to stay out of sight," Leo said through gritted teeth.

"And miss the big day. Not a chance," the man said. He was now right in front of them.

"Go do something else. I'll take care of this," the man told Leo.

She wanted to reach out and tell Leo not to leave her, but that would be overstepping what she was allowed to do.

"I don't think that's a good idea, Carl," Leo said.

The man, Carl, wasn't too happy with that answer.

"Who's in charge here, Leo?" he snapped.

"You are, Boss, but the master wants her ready and in his room in an hour — untouched," Leo told him.

The man glared at Leo before reaching for Elena. She couldn't help the squeak of fear from escaping her tight throat when Carl yanked her to him.

"It really is too bad. I should have never given up this one," he snarled. Then he crushed his lips to hers while grabbing her behind and pulling her against his body.

She shuddered when he released her.

"Okay, okay, you've made your point," Leo told him.

Carl simply laughed before he walked away. Elena was shaking when Leo faced her.

"I'm sorry, Elena," he told her as he put a dollop of cream in his hand. "Turn around."

It was the kindest she'd ever heard his voice. Still shaking, she presented her back to him, and he began rubbing the cream into her skin, instantly soothing all the places Carl had touched.

"I know him," she said in a small voice.

"Yeah, he never allowed you to see him before, but now he feels it's safe," Leo told her.

"Safe from what?" she asked. Her entire body was shaking.

"It doesn't matter, Elena. I'm just sorry you have to see him now."

"But I remember," she said on a sob. "I remember a whip."

Leo was quiet for several moments. He shook his head, seeming ashamed. She didn't understand.

"Before you were injured, he didn't show his face. You were masked. You're mixing images in your head now. It's better for you not to crack that door open," he warned.

Elena wanted to argue, but she been trained not to. She wanted to question Leo more, but she knew her place, knew she couldn't do that. She nodded at him and allowed him to do what he had to do. She didn't know any other way.

The process took about fifteen minutes and then she had to stand there a while longer while the lotion worked its magic. When Leo left the room and retuned holding several items, she looked at him with doubt.

"What is that?"

"It's what you're wearing," he told her. She couldn't tell from his tone what he thought about the outfit. She looked at the thigh-high boots with five-inch heels.

She'd been made to practice walking in heels, but these were huge.

"Stand still." She did as he asked as he pulled up a garter belt that rested low on her hips with little clasps hanging down.

"Sit down now."

Once she sat, he rolled the stockings onto her legs and attached them to the garter belt, and then he placed the boots on her feet and zipped them up.

"Stand up. See how they feel," he said.

She carefully stood and took a couple of steps. It wasn't easy, but she could at least walk.

"Where's the rest?" she asked him, feeling increasingly more cold with all her skin on display.

"That's all there is," he said.

She'd been naked a lot, was used to it. But they were moving through the house.

"Can I have a robe?" she tentatively asked.

"I'm sorry, Elena, but no. Let's get going."

He moved to the door, and she stood her ground. Elena wanted to refuse to follow him. Especially after seeing the man who had been a large part of her nightmares. This place might not be what she'd thought it was.

Was she truly free? Leo said he had saved her, and though she had no memory beyond the past month, flashes would enter her mind, flashes of some life before. Had it truly been as bad as Leo told her it was? Or was he lying to her?

No. She shook her head. Her entire purpose was to please the master. She wanted to please the master, she assured herself. But if that were the case, why was she so scared? Elena didn't understand any of it.

"Elena, we have to go." This time his voice was firmer.

She knew she could fight him, but she also knew the punishment would be fast and painful. With her head bent down, she walked after Leo, her stomach hurling as they began walking up the steps from the basement. They crossed a path outside, making her body shiver. And then they were back in the house she'd been in just a short time ago.

They entered the room where she'd met the master, and she hung her head in shame when a woman looked up as she was dusting a shelf. The woman didn't make eye contact, but Elena could imagine what she was thinking.

They passed a couple other people as Leo marched her up the stairs into a wide hallway and then walked her down it. By the time he opened a huge door at the end of the hall, her feet hurt, and she was doing her best not to cry.

"We're here," Leo told her unnecessarily.

She looked around the monstrous room. It was done in all dark colors with black bedding on top of a four-post bed, black curtains, and dark brown hardwood floors. There was a hutch near the bed that Leo walked over to. An image of something terrible happening in that bed flashed through her mind. She wanted to back away, run. But she was trained not to do that.

"Lie down in the middle of the bed and spread out your limbs," Leo said.

"I don't want to do this, Leo," she begged, her entire body beginning to shake.

"You don't have a choice, Elena," he said with a sigh. "Please don't fight me. I have to get this done."

He didn't even look her way as he opened the hutch, and she saw contraptions hanging there that terrified her. Elena decided she didn't care about the punishment. She couldn't do this. She turned and took several steps toward the door, but she was quickly swept off her feet.

"Dammit, Elena, don't do this," Leo growled.

He was holding a rope in his hand as he tossed her on the bed. She bounced and immediately struggled to move, to get away. But Leo was there and within seconds he had one of her hands secured to the post on the bed. He moved quickly and secured her other one.

"Please, Leo. I don't want to do this," she cried out again, her head thrashing as he moved to the bottom of the bed and secured both her feet.

"I know, Elena. But don't fight it. It will only make things worse. Just get through this. The first time will be the worst, and then it won't be so bad after that. But only if you don't fight the master. He wants you to fight him so he has an excuse to hurt you worse than he already plans on doing."

"Please, Leo, please don't let this happen," she sobbed, tears falling down her cheeks as her head thrashed.

"None of us have a choice," Leo said before shooting her a glare. "I never bothered to care much until you, dammit!"

"What do you mean?" She calmed herself as she looked at him.

"You fought so hard," he said, his voice quieting down. "You didn't want to give up. I think somewhere in there, you still . . ." He stopped talking and shook his head. "It doesn't matter."

Then he moved toward her, and the room went dark as a blindfold was placed over her eyes. She could scream or cry out but she knew it wouldn't do any good.

So instead of doing that, Elena shut her mind off. She shut everything off. She heard Leo leave and then she lay there and tried to completely blank her mind. Whatever was coming next wasn't going to be pleasant. If she could somehow take her mind somewhere else, then the master would have nothing except her body. Her body didn't matter. He could have that.

Time stopped having any meaning as she tuned in to the sound of a clock ticking. She squirmed on the bed as her arms and legs grew numb. She listened for the door to reopen, but it never did.

Shivering as she waited for the master, she tried telling herself that she would rather just get this night over with. But the longer she lay on the cold bed, the more terrified she became.

Elena began to drift to sleep when she was rudely reawakened by the sound of the bedroom door opening and footsteps entering the room.

CHAPTER TWENTY-ONE

SHIVERING IN THE middle of the bed, Elena lay there, not sure what to do. The door had opened, and there were steps and then . . . nothing.

She wanted to scream, but what good would that do her? There were more steps, but this time they were moving away from her. Was this all part of the plan? Did the master want her freaked out?

If he did, it was working.

She told herself over and over again it didn't matter. None of this mattered. But it did. She didn't know why, but somehow it mattered — *she* mattered.

As she was beginning to hyperventilate, she heard voices quietly speaking. She strained her ears to hear what they were saying.

". . . how many are left?"

"Just this one, Sir." That was Leo. The other voice she didn't recognize.

"What does she know?" the man asked.

"Nothing. She has vague memories once in a while. Otherwise, she's not a risk. After the coma she fully integrated into Elena."

There was silence as if the man was trying to comprehend that. What were they talking about? She was so confused.

"Now that my father is gone she has no risks." The man stopped.

"I truly am sorry for your loss, Sir."

"I'm not. He was an evil bastard, and he got what he deserved. If he hadn't been drinking and driving he never would have driven off the cliff. But he's gone now, and I have a hell of a mess to clean up after him."

Gone? Was the man who'd insisted she be tied to his bed gone? Unbelievable joy radiated through her. But before she could become too excited the men continued speaking.

"What do you want me to do?" Leo asked.

"You, I trust. None of the other men involved with any of this are trustworthy. I want them given a settlement. You'll meet with Stephan, and he will write the checks; have them sign the nondisclosure agreements, and I want them off the property within the hour, all access cut off."

"Yes, Sir," Leo replied.

"What about the other men, the ones who find the girls?" the man asked.

"They have no idea who they are working for. They've always been met far away," Leo assured him.

"That's good. We don't have that mess to clean up. I've spent too long building this company after my father failed it on so many levels. I won't let his transgressions bring it down. It hasn't been his for a very long time," the man said.

"We all know that, Sir," Leo told him.

There was silence and then she heard the steps coming closer to the bed. She shook as she waited for whatever her fate might be. Should she pretend to be asleep? If they were speaking so openly, would that mean they were planning on disposing of her?

"Cover her up," the man growled.

Elena felt covers go over her body, and she fought not to give a grateful thank you to the man. Yes, her body wasn't her own anymore, but that didn't mean she enjoyed being laid out on display.

"What do we do here, Sir?" Leo asked again.

"I don't know, Leo." The man sighed. "Let's talk to her."

Suddenly the mask was removed from Elena's eyes, and she blinked as she adjusted to the bright light. Then she sucked in her breath as she got her first look at the man staring down at her.

She said nothing.

"What's your name?" he asked.

Suddenly her throat closed, and she wasn't able to respond. She looked at him like a deer caught in headlights.

"I asked a question," the man said, taking a step closer.

"Elena," she finally whispered.

"I'm Dalton, Elena. I'm sorry you've been tied up here for so long. The man you met earlier was my father. He and I don't share the same views on how people should be treated. If I have Leo release you from these binds are you going to fight me?"

"No. I promise I won't," she told him.

"How old are you?" he asked, his eyes never straying past hers, though she was now covered.

"I think I'm eighteen," she said, her voice very quiet.

"Dammit!" Dalton stepped away from the bed as he paced the room.

"I'm sorry," she said, not knowing why she was apologizing, but just knowing she'd somehow upset the man.

"There's nothing to apologize for," he said, the words coming out harshly. She decided to keep her mouth shut.

"How long has she been here?" This time the question was directed at Leo. She was curious about this herself. She'd never had a direct answer on that question. She could only remember back a little while.

Leo's back was turned to her, and she didn't see his lips move when he told Dalton that answer. But it must not have pleased the man because he swore again before moving back over to her.

Leo finished untying her, and Elena immediately began rubbing her tender wrists before she gripped the edges of the blanket and slowly sat up. Her body ached from being secured in one place for so long. Had it been hours? Certainly. She just wasn't sure exactly how long. Blood rushed through her limbs, sending tingling sensations throughout.

"Where do you live, Elena?" Dalton asked.

She slowly shook her head. "I don't know," she finally admitted.

Dalton swore again. "This is a mess," he thundered.

"We can have her work here, Sir," Leo suggested. "I think it would be best for all concerned if we gave her a place to stay."

Leo didn't face her as he spoke.

"I don't think we have much choice in the matter," Dalton answered.

What were they talking about? Elena wanted to ask, but she was incredibly confused. Dalton moved back to the bed, and this time he sat down on the edge. Everything in Elena wanted to scoot away, but she was afraid of the retaliation if she did so. The man didn't touch her though. That was somewhat of a relief.

"Have you been mistreated?" Dalton asked.

Elena's eyes widened as her head whipped around toward Leo and then back to Dalton. She didn't know how to answer that without things becoming a whole lot worse for her.

Finally she shook her head again. "No, Sir."

His dark eyes bored into hers, and she wanted to flinch under his knowing gaze, but she managed to maintain eye contact.

"I have a feeling you aren't telling me the whole truth," he finally said, the barest of smiles touching his lips. "Any abuse you've endured won't continue."

Relief rushed through Elena, and then, all of a sudden, she looked at Dalton in a different way. With fear leaving her, she took the time to notice this man who casually sat there and spoke almost kindly to her.

He had nearly black eyes with thick dark lashes, giving him an exotic look. She wasn't sure of his age, but he appeared to be maybe late twenties, and he was huge, like the other man, his father, but without all the softness. He stood well above six foot, and his shoulders were twice as wide as hers. Not that she had much shoulders at all. So maybe his were three times as wide.

His mouth was frowning again, but his face was attractive, if she were capable of being attracted to a man. She feared men right now more than anything else. But he had a square jaw, high cheekbones, and a perfectly straight nose. There was something about him that drew her to him. She forgot Leo was even standing in the room as she gazed at this man sitting so close to her.

"You're going to work for me, Elena," he finally said.

"Okay," she replied, not even thinking of arguing.

"I'll have Leo supervise you. You won't leave the grounds."

He waited for a response. She hadn't even contemplated leaving the grounds. She knew the area she was allowed to walk in. But as long as they continued letting her outside, she could handle almost anything. Well, anything except being tied to a bed for hours on end.

"Do you understand this?" Dalton asked, seeming irritated that she hadn't given him a reply.

"Yes, Sir," she quickly answered.

"Good." He then turned to Leo. "Get her covered and out of this room. I want the entire thing stripped. I don't want a single reminder of my father left in this house."

"Are you moving back home, Sir?" Leo asked.

He paused again as he looked down at Elena. She couldn't read his eyes, but then she wasn't good at reading people since she didn't even know who she was. Finally he turned back to Leo.

"For now. Until I get this mess straightened out," he replied.

With that, the man stood up and walked out. Elena didn't budge from her place on the bed, huddled beneath the blanket.

"It looks like the rough times are over, Elena," Leo said, not too unkindly.

"Can I go back to my room now?"

"Yes, let's get those boots off you first," he said with almost a smile.

"I can do it," she told him, expecting him to argue.

"Well, get on it. I want out of this room."

She quickly undid the boots, and then wrapped the blanket around her and followed Leo out. Relief washed through her when she made it back to her small room. Somehow her prayers had been answered.

At least that's how it felt. She didn't remember her life before this place, so this was as good as it got.

CHAPTER TWENTY-TWO

A NEW DAY CAME and Elena sat in her room wondering what to do. She had no idea. The master was dead — was never going to return. Did that mean Dalton was now in charge of her? Was Leo? She really didn't know. She felt lost, which wasn't exactly a new feeling, but not knowing her place was something she didn't know how to deal with.

Her stomach rumbled in hunger, but still she sat and waited for further instruction. An hour passed, and then two. She squirmed with the need to use the restroom and find something to eat. Was she simply going to be left alone in her room all day? If no one came, she'd have to decide if she was capable of making her own decision.

Thinking on her own was so pounded out of her, it felt wrong to even have as simple of a thought as to get up and take care of her basic needs. When no one came after another hour passed, Elena was left with no choice but to rise from where she sat huddled on her bed.

She slowly walked across the short space in her room to the door and opened it, then walked into the hallway and looked around. Not a sound could be heard from either direction. First things first, she went to the restroom, taking her time as she brushed her teeth and bathed. It felt wonderful to shower without other hands scraping against her body. A smile almost flitted across her lips.

When she finished, she wrapped a towel around her and went back to her room where only a few changes of clothes sat in the small two-drawer dresser. She put on an outfit offering her the most protection, then slowly moved to the stairs that led to the shed above. Leo was normally there to tell her she could go up, but he hadn't yet come, and she was so hungry.

Her limbs trembling, she made her way up the stairs, opening the door at the top, finding herself in the shed that covered the underground basement. She'd been allowed to walk this path many times to the backdoor of the mansion where there was a separate servants entrance, and a small kitchen area for staff members. That's where she'd eaten when food wasn't brought to her in the basement.

She looked around before stepping outside, and then made the decision to go to the house. Terror filled her, because if she was doing something wrong, she knew it wouldn't go well for her. Reaching the house she stood there for minutes trying to decide if she should go inside or not.

The decision was taken from her when the door suddenly pushed open. Elena took a step back, wishing she hadn't stepped out of line, wishing she would have just waited in her small room for someone to come. Looking up in fright she found Leo moving down the stairs before he glanced up and saw her.

"I'm sorry," she quickly said, averting her gaze. "No one came and I was hungry."

On the verge of tears, she shook where she stood, waiting to know what her punishment would be for doing something without being told it was okay.

Leo moved over to her, and surprised her when he wrapped his arms around her and carefully pulled her in close for a hug that took her breath away. He was such a big man that it didn't take much pressure from his arms to squeeze her.

"Don't apologize, Elena. It's my fault," he told her. He leaned down and kissed her forehead in a comforting gesture. "There was a lot to get done today and I didn't realize how much time had passed."

"I should have waited," she said.

"The rules have changed, little one. Dalton isn't the same man as his father. You will get a lot more freedom now. If you're hungry, you are more than free to come to the kitchen and get food. If you want to take a walk around the property in the areas you know you're allowed, you can do that too. You will have a work schedule that we're going to go over after you've had some food, but when you aren't working, your time is your own," he assured her.

Elena replayed his words in her mind as she tried to understand them. She'd never been allowed freedom before. Leo had told her it was just the way it was, that he didn't make up the rules, but still, it was so ingrained in her, that she didn't know what to do with these changes in circumstance. It was almost too much for her to comprehend or want.

"I'm scared, Leo," she told him.

"I know you are. I'm sorry about that," he said with a sigh. He released her and took a step back so he could see her face. Elena fought back the urge to cry. At least when Leo was telling her what to do, she had a clear understanding of where she stood. Now, that was all changing.

"What if I mess up?" she asked him.

"It will take some time to adjust to this new way of life, but I assure you, it will all be much better," he told her. His fingers caressed her cheek, and she felt comforted.

"Thank you for not leaving me, Leo," she told him. She wanted to reach for him, to take comfort in another one of his gentle embraces, but it wasn't her place to do that.

He smiled kindly at her. "I've wanted to save you for a very long time. I was too afraid to do that, and I'm filled with remorse for it every single day. But even in spite of my weakness, you are now free in a way that wasn't possible before. You can finally grow up and I will be there every step of the way with you."

"I don't know what I would do without you, Leo."

The two of them had spoken many times, but never had she felt it acceptable to say these sort of things to him. It felt freeing and she realized she had a friend in him. It was odd to think such a thought.

"I guess we need each other, little one," he said with a smile. "How about we feed you and then I can tell you more about your new life?" he suggested.

Her stomach rumbled as he said that and she smiled. Her cheeks felt the sting of muscles not often used and she wondered how bad her life had been before the coma that she hadn't felt like smiling. Maybe Leo would trust her enough to tell her if she concentrated and did a really good job with her work.

She followed him to the kitchen and it was just the two of them as they sat at the table and she ate toast and eggs while he sipped on coffee. Leo went over the new rules with her, and instead of her being trained and prepped for the master, now she would clean and have assigned hours she worked, and even one day a week that was all for herself.

It was more than she ever could have imagined. If Elena could understand what joy felt like, she would think that's what she was feeling. It was amazing. She smiled at Leo and watched as something in his eyes sparkled. She didn't know what that meant.

"I'm glad to see you smiling, Elena. Your entire face lights up. You should do it a lot more often," he told her.

"I don't think I had a lot of reason to smile before. I don't know why, but my cheeks hurt from doing it today so that tells me it probably wasn't something I did before my accident," she said.

Leo flinched the slightest bit before he was able to school his expression. She wanted to ask him about it, but it probably didn't matter.

"We all make mistakes in life, Elena. I urge you to quit scratching at the block in your head. If there's a wall up, it's there for a reason, and it might devastate you to discover the memories that are behind it," he told her.

That made a lot of sense, Elena realized. Why would Leo lie to her anyway? He'd been nothing but kind to her for as long as she could remember. Sure, he'd had to punish her a few times, but that had only happened because it was his job — what he'd had to do. He'd always told her he was sorry, but it was necessary to prepare her for the master.

She understood.

"I've been trained for as long as I can remember to be a certain way for the master. Now that he's gone, I don't really understand what I'm supposed to do," she told him.

Leo was quiet for so long that she wondered if she'd offended him with what she'd just said. The last thing she wanted to do was make the man who'd been so good to her angry or upset. She said nothing as she waited.

"I should have gotten you out of here a long time ago. But there's no need to think of the past and make wishes on what should have been done. We just have to move forward now. You will find your place in this world, and I'll be by your side the entire time," he told her.

Elena again smiled as she looked at him. "Thank you, Leo. I couldn't ask for anything else than just that," she told him.

He reached for her hands and clasped her fingers in his. The gesture felt exactly right and she felt safe. Elena didn't feel a lot of emotions on a day-to-day basis. She'd been taught she wasn't allowed to think or feel for herself. So it was odd to feel such strong emotions in this moment. But Leo had assured her that her life was changing. Maybe it was time to embrace this for what it was — a new day and a new life.

"I have a lot I'm supposed to do. I don't want to be a disappointment on my new first day," she said as she glanced down at the notes she'd been taking while Leo filled her in on her new duties.

"You aren't a disappointment at all. Let me help you get started. I'll be keeping an eye on you, but the head housekeeper will be your boss," he told her.

"Okay," she said, complete trust in Leo.

He gave her another look that she couldn't quite understand, but Elena knew she didn't need to comprehend it all. If she did as she was instructed, things should run smoothly. That was really all that mattered in the end. She cleaned up her breakfast dishes and followed Leo. She'd probably follow him anywhere. He was the one who had saved her after-all.

What she didn't understand was why, even as she had this thought, a flash of Dalton ran through her mind. He'd come when the master should have been in his place, and he'd made her feel something she'd never felt before. But he was nothing to her, not someone she should think about at all. So why she'd be having kind thoughts about Leo only to then think about Dalton, she didn't know.

Elena was sure it was only because she was incredibly messed up. There was no other explanation for it. Maybe time would help heal the many wounds she was sure were buried deep down inside her. She hoped the wall Leo spoke of never did come tumbling down. He was probably right in that it was best for her to leave it firmly in place.

With it right where it should be she didn't have to remember those flashes of memories that tried sneaking up on her that only spoke of pain and suffering. She could picture her life how she wanted it to be instead of how it was. That was better — she had no doubt it was much, much better.

CHAPTER TWENTY-THREE

TIME STOPPED HAVING any meaning to Elena. One day would simply meld into another and then another. She worked, cleaning the house, and she enjoyed her freedom to step outside in the evenings, but she did nothing other than that.

She didn't see Dalton again. When he was home, only a few of the fully trusted staff were allowed in his area. The rest of them, including her, were banished to the slave quarters, as she called them.

She'd asked Leo if she would ever leave, and he had shaken his head, told her there was too much at stake for that. If there were any visitors in the house, she was not only banished to the slave quarters, but she was also locked up.

Elena didn't understand why. Were they afraid of her doing something? Did they think she was so uncivilized she wouldn't know how to behave around normal humans? Once in a while she would still watch the videos that were in the sitting room. The other servants slept somewhere else on the grounds. She was alone in her small domain.

Elena didn't understand any of it. Her memory had never come back, but she still had a reoccurring dream with a little boy whose face was always blurry, but his blond hair was crystal clear. She so wanted to meet him. Though she didn't understand why.

As more time passed, she stopped longing for something else, longing for something she knew nothing of. This was the life she'd been given; it was the life she would have to accept.

A new head housekeeper had been hired a few months ago, and he was a horrible man. Not as bad as the one who'd been there so long ago, the one who had enjoyed hurting her, but this housekeeper, who was only referred to as Ken, would slap her if he wasn't satisfied with her work.

Elena was used to that, though. She knew better than to complain. When she dwelled too much on things like that, it would make her sad, depressingly miserable, so she chose not to focus on it. What good did it do her?

It was a warm day and she was in the living room, her work flawless — at least, she felt it was. She didn't see confrontation coming, but suddenly she was on the ground, the sting of Ken's slap leaving a red mark on her cheek.

"What do you think you're doing?"

"I . . . I'm cleaning," she told him.

She was used to the pain, but still, being hit in the face knocked her for a loop.

"You call this clean?" the man thundered.

"What am I doing wrong?" she asked.

"Everything! I don't understand why you're still around," he snapped as he ran his gloved finger over the surface she'd been dusting. She didn't see anything on his spotless glove, but he looked at his finger in disgust.

"You won't eat lunch today. Redo this entire room." With that, he turned and walked out.

Most days, Elena would simply begin her work again, redo a job that was already impeccable, but this wasn't one of those days. She was at a breaking point.

She crawled into the corner, allowing a random moment of self-pity as she wrapped her knees close to her chest and sat there with tears streaming down her cheeks. She wouldn't allow this pity party to continue for long. If she was caught, the consequences were just too great. It wasn't worth it. Finally, she pulled herself together and stood.

And that's when she realized she was no longer alone.

Standing in the doorway, Dalton was watching her. She couldn't tell from his expression what he was thinking. But like the first time she'd seen him, her breath was taken away.

He'd changed in the past few months. His jaw was firmer, his shoulders a little wider, his eyes, oh his eyes, were hard. But when she looked at him, the first thing that came to her mind was he'd saved her from a fate she hadn't been able to comprehend.

"I'm so sorry. I didn't realize you'd be in here," she told him, quickly averting her eyes. She wasn't allowed to look at him, if ever she did happen to be in the same room.

If Ken found out about this, she would be punished severely, even though it wasn't her fault. She was in the room she'd been assigned to. That didn't matter though. Whether it was her fault or not, she would be the one in trouble.

"Why are you crying?"

His voice was so controlled, so cold and hard. It sent a shiver down her spine. She feared this man, but not in the way she feared Ken, or any number of other people. She feared this man because there was something about him that she knew would break her in ways she'd never imagined being broken.

"It's nothing, Sir. I'm truly sorry. Let me get out of your way," she told him, not knowing if she should move and walk away or wait for him to exit the area first.

"I'll dismiss you when we're finished," he told her, his voice never modulating. "I asked you a question. I don't like to ask twice."

"I've not been doing my job well enough, and I was having a moment of self-pity. I promise you it won't happen again," she said, not wanting to face this man's wrath by not answering.

"Self-pity is for the weak," he firmly said.

"I know that, Sir. I'm very sorry."

She stood there, her eyes still averted to the ground. Everything inside her wanted to look up, wanted to see what his expression was, but she knew better than that. In her months of having more freedom, she had grown. She still felt fear run through her, but she was gaining more backbone. It was something she didn't fully understand.

"You've changed," he finally said, his voice a tad softer.

"I don't know what you mean," she said.

"Look at me," he commanded.

Her head came up. She wouldn't refuse. He began moving toward her, and her stomach tightened in panic. She had the urge to turn and run, but she wasn't allowed to do that. She stood right where she was as he slowly approached.

Lifting his hand he cupped her chin and tilted her head from side to side as he examined her. "Yes, you've changed — grown," he murmured. Was that surprise she saw in his expression?

"I guess I have," she finally said, unsure what he was wanting from her.

"There's no guessing about it," he almost whispered, his eyes darkening the tiniest bit. "Are you being treated well?"

He'd asked her something like this the first time she'd met him. She was still unwilling to tell him the truth.

"Very well, Sir."

His lip turned up the slightest bit as his eyes held hers captive. "I see you still lie," he said in a mocking tone.

Then as if her touch were burning him, he quickly released her and took a step back, his expression turning back to the cold look she'd first witnessed in his telling eyes.

"I'll take care of it."

With that, he turned and walked away.

Elena wanted to call after him, ask him what he planned on doing, but she stood frozen to the spot he'd left her.

What was he going to do? And what would be her punishment because of it? Her knees shook as she looked around the spotless room. Ken had told her to redo the entire thing, but she could barely stand, her knees were shaking so badly.

The first time she'd met Dalton, she'd been afraid but drawn to the man in a way she couldn't comprehend. This time, he'd been like a magnetic force. She'd wanted to run, but she'd also wanted to stay right there with him.

What was wrong with her? Why couldn't she think for herself? The encounter had made her weak in the knees, and her heart was racing. There was something so controlled about him, something that drew her to him.

Maybe it was because she always felt like she was spinning out of control, maybe that was why she wanted to be in his aura, to feel like her feet were firmly planted on the ground. Whatever it was, she had no business feeling this way.

Looking around the room one more time, Elena decided this was a good time to make her exit. Ken wouldn't be able to tell if she'd re-cleaned. It was already immaculate.

Moving swiftly, she made her way to her dungeon and sat on her bed. Without thinking about it, her fingers lifted and caressed her cheek where Dalton's fingers had caressed her. It felt as if the skin had been burned.

She would do well not to think such thoughts. But when hardly anyone ever spoke to her, let alone offered her even a moment of kindness, it was difficult not to dwell upon the one good moment.

That night, Elena fell asleep and dreamed of Dalton. When she awoke, she was feeling things inside of her she didn't understand and couldn't possibly comprehend. But she ached; her entire body ached.

What was worse, she wanted to see Dalton again . . .

CHAPTER TWENTY-FOUR

THE SUN WAS just setting, and Elena had a favorite spot in the garden where she liked to watch it dip below the trees. She leaned back against the log, watching the sky fill with oranges and purples.

Her stress fell away as she took in the brilliant colors. There was something about the sky darkening that made her feel like a new day would take away all her worries. She didn't know what it was, but any time she was done with her chores early she would rush outside to this same place and sit for over an hour, feeling her body relax.

"I thought I would find you here."

The deep baritone startled her, making Elena's relaxed body shoot up as she gazed over at the hulking man walking toward her.

"Am I not supposed to be here?" she asked. No one had ever had a problem with it before.

"I've just noticed you like routine. You come out here almost nightly," Dalton told her. She began to rise. "Sit back."

The words were a command. She had no doubt about it. Her body was no longer relaxed as she sat a bit straighter, bringing her knees up to her chest and hugging them while he walked closer, and then surprised her by sitting down next to her.

She couldn't imagine a man in such impeccable clothing dropping down on the ground. His suit jacket hung open, showing her his crisp white shirt and loosened tie. His five o'clock shadow gave him a mysterious look.

The sun was all the way down now, leaving the two of them in the shadows of the shade trees, and she squirmed beside him not knowing exactly what it was he wanted from her.

"I've been trying to stay away from you," he said, as if answering her question.

"Oh." She paused for a long moment, unsure what she was supposed to say to that. "I'm sorry if I've been in your way," she finally added.

She held her breath when he turned, his body now facing her while he stretched out his hand to run through her hair.

"You have nothing to be sorry about, Elena," he said, his tone hushed. "There's something about you . . ." His words trailed off as his fingers tightened in her hair.

The breath she'd been holding finally exploded free, breaking the sudden silence.

"Do you know why I'm sitting here with you?" he asked, his fingers moving to her neck.

She shivered as his fingers caressed her. There were strange flutters in her stomach and suddenly her nipples were aching. What in the world was going on?

"No," she finally said when she knew he expected her to say something.

"You have no idea how attractive you are, do you?" Though it was a question, she could see he was simply voicing his thoughts aloud. She didn't understand why he was speaking to her this way. They'd barely seen each other, let alone spoken more than a few words.

"No, you're obviously innocent, *despite* being here. Maybe that's why I'm drawn to you," he told her, his fingers moving down her shoulder, his fingertips running along her arm.

Goosebumps appeared on her flesh, and she sat wide-eyed while he drank his fill of her. She'd never been caressed before. Every inch of her body had been beaten, touched, and fondled, but no one had ever made her feel what she was feeling right at this moment.

A flash of people naked, grunting, and moaning on the screen in the media room flashed before her eyes, and she shook her head trying to focus on the memory, but just as soon as the image started up in her brain, it quickly fluttered away. There was nothing she could remember before waking up in that bed with Leo next to her.

Leo had touched her a lot, but never like this, and never while looking into her eyes with the look Dalton was currently giving her. Should she tell him she had to go in now? She never disobeyed orders, and he hadn't told her she could leave yet.

The funny thing was, she didn't want to leave.

Her lips were dry. But when her tongue came out and moistened them, Dalton's eyes narrowed the slightest bit and his mouth opened. The look made her stomach flutter all the more.

Without another word, his hand came to rest against her neck, this time not so gently, as he held her in place and then leaned forward. When his lips found hers, she didn't know what to do. She'd been kissed by some of the men in this house; they'd told her she had to know how to do it right, but never before had a burst of heat surged through her at the touch of their lips on hers.

Dalton was confident as he pulled her onto his lap and took the kiss to a new level, pushing past her lips and thrusting his tongue inside her mouth while his fingers wound through her hair. He straddled her across his lap and surged his hips up so she felt hardness press against the V of her thighs.

She felt wetness coat her as the surge of electricity running through her body intensified. He deepened the kiss for a moment before pulling back.

"I should let you go," he murmured, his lips only an inch from hers, making it impossible for her to see clearly into his eyes.

Let her go? Had she done something wrong? Elena was powerless as Dalton's hands continued sliding up and down her back. This entire experience seemed almost otherworldly. It was odd. This was the sort of thing she'd been trained to do with the master. But it had been months since that man was gone, and she hadn't thought about it in so long, she didn't understand exactly what was going on.

Dalton was now her owner, the one who controlled her, but he hadn't done anything that caused her fear. And the warm feelings growing inside her only caused more confusion. She didn't understand what he meant by letting her go. She wasn't sure she wanted to.

"I don't know why I'm still keeping you here," he said again, his warm breath washing over her. At those words, she felt panic invade her.

"Have I displeased you?" she asked, afraid of his answer.

She could swear she saw shock in his gaze, but that wasn't a look she'd ever seen directed at her before, so she was sure she was reading him correctly. Elena had been trained to be the perfect girl, not to speak her own mind, so how could she possibly shock the man?

"No, Elena. The problem is you please me a little too much, and I know how wrong that is," he said with a sigh. He leaned forward again and pressed his lips to hers. There was no urge for her to pull away from him, nothing inside her that revolted at what he was doing. She found that she wanted to press closer to him, even if she didn't exactly understand why.

She knew what sex was, had been trained on how to accept what was her duty — her responsibility in pleasing a man. What she didn't understand was her body's reaction to what Dalton was doing to her. She had felt nothing like it when others had kissed her, and thrust their grimy fingers all over her body.

Dalton's mouth was firm and confident. He easily opened her lips and she turned her head as his fingers sank more fully into her hair, tugging her strands to hold her in place. The small pinch of pain didn't even register as he pushed his hips upward against the softness between her thighs. A growing ache spread through her that was almost more painful than a slap.

When he pulled back again, she was panting as her eyes opened and she gazed into the black depths of his eyes. There was a look in them that frightened and excited her all at once. He growled low in his throat and she sighed. Everything he was doing made her want to be like the women she'd watched on the large television in the basement. She wanted to please this man if he needed her to do so.

"I need to let you go," he said once more, anger now in his voice. That was an emotion Elena knew quite well. She spoke before thinking of stopping herself.

"I don't have anywhere to go," she whispered. She wasn't sure if he was talking about *this* moment in his arms, or for her to leave his property, but either option terrified her.

He leaned in and sucked her bottom lip into his mouth for a brief moment before releasing it and then he lifted her from his lap. The ache she felt at the loss of his touch was almost unbearable. Elena had felt true pain and to compare it with how she was feeling at Dalton's abandonment shocked her. But she couldn't think of anything else to describe how she was feeling other than bereft and … damaged somehow.

In all the time she'd been able to remember at being at this property, and with everything she'd gone through, Elena hadn't hoped for anything. She couldn't even remember wanting freedom. But as Dalton gazed down at her, she found herself yearning for him to want her.

"I know you have nowhere else to go, he said." She'd almost forgotten her last spoken words, it had taken him so long to respond. But then he stood up and her eyes trailed to his pants where a large bulge was obvious.

He seemed to notice her look because he groaned. Her eyes shot up to his, and he took another step back.

"I'm going straight to hell," he murmured.

He said nothing else as he turned and walked away.

Elena didn't move for maybe an hour. She wasn't sure her legs could hold her up. She didn't know what to think about what had just happened. All she knew was she'd been kissed for the first time that hadn't revolted her.

Finally, she got up and stumbled to the safety of her room. Her legs were like rubber as she made her way down the steps and her lips still tingled from where Dalton's had pressed against them. She went on autopilot as she got into her pajamas and climbed into bed. However, sleep was the last thing on her mind. All her thoughts were focused on Dalton and the strange feelings he had inspiring inside her.

If only there was someone she could talk to, share with, ask advice of. But there was no one. And Elena knew there never would be a person. Somehow she was smart enough to know better than to bring any of this up to Leo. He would be so disappointed in her and to ever do anything that would make him unhappy scared Elena.

Elena wasn't so foolish as to believe Leo was her friend. He was her boss, and a boss could never be a friend. He'd told her that once. But he also expected her to obey him and the rules of the house. How she was feeling about Dalton was a clear violation of any rules that had been laid out for her.

Tossing in her bed, Elena whimpered, the sound drifting off into nothingness. She just hated so much that she was experiencing these feelings and had no way of knowing how to understand them.

Maybe someday she would know who she was, maybe then she could understand all of this. But for now, she tossed in her bed, and when sleep finally did come to her, so did Dalton . . . if only in her dreams.

CHAPTER TWENTY-FIVE

ONE DAY WAS really the same as another in this place. Each night Elena had dreams, images flashing in her mind, pictures of people that sent a tingling sensation through her brain, tickled the fibers there, but unable to tear down the protective wall Leo assured her she didn't want to rip away.

Though she knew it was better not to let the memories in, she still found herself wanting to know the faces flashing before her eyes. She needed to understand who she was. All she could remember was being trained, prepped, made to serve another. With her new bit of freedom, she felt as if there were more to life than just being a servant.

Lying in her bed, she heard footsteps outside her door, but it didn't cause her alarm. The only one who came down to the basement was Leo. He wouldn't hurt her — he cared about her, was her friend.

There was a tapping on her bedroom door before it was pushed open. Then the light from the hallway was blocked as Leo's large body took up the entire space. She gave him a sleepy smile as he stepped forward.

"Am I late?" she asked him as she stretched her arms out and yawned. Her dreams from the night before had been particularly engaging and she was having a difficult time coming back to reality.

"Not at all. Today is your day off so I thought we could have a picnic," he said as he held up a basket.

"What's a picnic?" she asked.

Leo looked stunned at the question for a minute and then he laughed. His face transformed with the merry sound and Elena couldn't help but smile with him. She'd never seen Leo in such a good mood.

"I forget sometimes that you have amnesia and can't remember everything," he told her as he moved closer and sat down on her bed. "A picnic is a tradition where people pack a lunch and sit down on the ground to eat while enjoying the weather."

"That sounds wonderful," she told him. "Do you think I've had them before?"

Leo was still smiling, but slowly it began to fade as he reached out and ran his finger down her cheek. While the gesture was comforting, Elena wondered at why it didn't give her the same feeling as when Dalton touched her. Was it because Leo had been the one to train her, to have to punish her sometimes?

She didn't know.

"I know it's frustrating that you can't remember your past, and that you think it would be so much better for you if you took down the wall. Yes, it would be nice to know simple things like what a picnic is, but I promise you, Elena, it's not worth it. The pain you have gone through will rip your very soul apart," Leo told her.

His fingers sifted through her hair and she looked at him with utter trust. He was the one who hadn't ever lied to her. She knew she had no other choice but to trust him and to listen to what he told her.

"I can't help the dreams, Leo," she told him. "I don't ask for them, don't want images of people and other things to keep flashing in my head. I can't stop it," she told him, her voice apologetic.

"I know, little one, I know," he said.

He leaned down and kissed her forehead before sitting back up and looking at her with what seemed like adoration in his gaze. Elena wondered if this was love — if she loved Leo. She had no idea what the emotion felt like, but she knew she felt protected by him, knew she was happier when he was there.

But she also didn't feel that odd sensation in strange places of her body when he touched her, comforted her, kissed her skin. She just felt safe.

"Are you happy, Elena?" he asked, surprising her.

It wasn't a question she could ever remember being asked. She opened her mouth to tell him that of course she was, but no words came out. Elena didn't know if she was happy, or for that matter, what happiness even was. Leo lay down next to her and pulled her up against him, his large arm holding her close.

She leaned her head against his chest; the sound of his heart beating against her ear was rhythmic and soothing. Leo had touched every part of her body and he'd pulled her in for hugs, kissed her forehead, smiled comfortingly at her, but he'd never laid in bed with her before.

Images of the videos flashed before her eyes and she remembered what she was expected to do while in a bed with a man. That made her body tense. What if Leo was expecting *that* from her? She felt a shiver of fear rush through at the thought and tensed.

Leo's hand smoothed its way up and down her back. She almost forgot about his question asking if she was happy. At this moment, she was scared everything familiar in her life was going to change. Happiness was the last thing on her mind.

"What's the matter, little one?" he asked, his warm breath cascading over the top of her head.

"Nothing," she said, but the tenseness of her muscles, he surely felt, called her a liar and she knew it.

"You can talk to me about anything," he assured her. "I've been with you every step of the way and I won't leave you."

His hand kept moving up and down her back, while his other one reached up and rubbed her head. He didn't speak again for several minutes and soon Elena let out a relieved breath. She didn't know why she'd been so worried. This was Leo, her savior, her friend. He wasn't like those men she'd watched in the videos; he would never hurt her.

"I don't really know what happiness is," she admitted, returning to his question from several minutes ago. "If I could understand it, I guess I would say that I'm happy."

"Don't worry about not understanding it," he told her with a chuckle. "Even people who don't have a block in their head, don't know what happiness is. I think it's something we all search for, but life gets so dang muddled that we end up not knowing what makes us truly happy and what we *think* makes us happy."

"Are you happy?" she asked.

He didn't speak for several moments, but his hands continued to gently move over her and she sunk a little bit more securely against him. She closed her eyes and took comfort in his touch and voice.

"I would have to say I don't know," he told her. "I think I have moments of happiness, but I also have a lot of time where I question every single decision in my life. I wonder how I get to one place or the other."

"Do you think if the wall ever comes down, that I will remember what makes me happy?" she asked.

"No," he said, his voice sure. "I think if the wall ever comes down, you'll remember why you ran away in the first place, remember more pain than you can imagine, and I think it will take away the ability for you to ever find happiness again."

"Then I don't ever want the wall to come down," she said with surety.

"I'm here to protect you, Elena. You don't need to remember things of the past that haunt you because you will always have me by your side," he told her.

"I don't know what I would do without you, Leo," she told him.

"I guess we're both a couple of broken souls and it's us against the world," he said with another chuckle. "I'm certainly glad you came into my life, Elena."

She didn't know what to say to that, so she kept silent as she listened to the slow and steady beat of Leo's heart. In this moment there wasn't any pain, or confusion. She was where she belonged.

Elena was sure her strange reaction to Dalton was because her head was so messed up. She wanted to ask Leo about it, wanted to question him and know if what she was feeling was right or wrong.

After all, Leo had been the one to teach her the way she should act for the master. Dalton was the master's son, and maybe he expected her to now be whatever Dalton wanted her to be. But for some reason Elena was afraid to question Leo about it.

Maybe it was because she no longer wanted to be a submissive, her only purpose in life to serve a man who could do whatever he wanted with her. Maybe now she wanted to discover what it was *she* liked and needed.

If she brought it up to Leo, maybe he would think she wanted to be that other girl — that girl who would be tied to a bed, whose soul purpose was to serve another. She knew she felt something for Dalton, she just wasn't sure what any of that meant.

Instead of bringing any of that up to Leo, she laid in his arms for a while longer, before finally the two of them rose and she went into the bathroom to get ready for the picnic with him.

The day was perfect. Leo made her laugh and relax, made her feel almost as if she had a place in this strange world she'd found herself in. She couldn't ask for anything more than that. He was a gentleman — nothing like the men on the videos she'd been forced to watch.

When she went to sleep that night it should have been Leo she dreamed about. But it wasn't. First, the blurry image of that little blonde boy who always seemed to come to her, flashed before her eyes. When he went away, she found herself in a meadow, flowers blooming all around her.

Elena spun in a circle as the warmth of the sun heated her cheeks, and the cool summer breeze took away the hotness of the day. The sound of her laughter rose high into the sky before she heard steps approaching.

When she turned, she saw Dalton walking toward her. His lips were firm, his eyes full of purpose. There was no slowing of his pace as he approached, and then he was standing in front of her.

Take off your clothes, he told her, his voice gruff.

Even in her sleep Elena fought against what he was requesting. But while her mind fought it, her body heated, trembles raced through her system.

I don't want to, she said.

His hard lips tilted up, a mocking look appearing in his eyes as he reached out and ran his fingers across her lips before trailing them down her chin and over the top of her breasts. He laughed — no mirth to the sound.

Yes you do, Elena. You want me even in your dreams, he told her.

Elena knew she should turn around and run. This was *her* dream and she should be able to choose which direction it was going. But her feet felt cemented to the ground. She couldn't pull herself away from the man. She closed her eyes and tried to take herself from this dream world she wasn't sure she wanted to leave.

When she opened them again, the meadow was gone. She was naked, lying in the bed she'd been in when Dalton had found her. She tried to move, but her arms and legs were secured, the boots on her feet. Dalton stood at the foot of the bed as he reached for the buttons on his crisp white shirt.

You're mine now, he told her, lust like what she'd seen in the videos gleaming in his eyes.

Instead of fear, Elena felt a deep sense of anticipation. She knew she shouldn't want this, but her heart pounded in her chest as she waited for him to give her a glimpse of his skin. A low moan escaped her lips, the sound shocking her. She closed her eyes, her head thrown back.

Something fell to the floor and Elena wrenched her eyes open, but Dalton was gone. She twisted her body and found she wasn't tied down; she wasn't in the master's bedroom. She was in her own small room, her body covered in a sheen of sweat, her heart pounding out of control.

Elena knew there was something wrong with her. Why would she have such a dream? Why did she have these thoughts in her head about a man? Her soul purpose had been to please the master, but then she'd been set free. Why wasn't she reaching for that freedom that was right there within her grasp?

Maybe because she was as messed up as Leo assured her she was. Maybe she truly didn't deserve freedom or happiness. Maybe it was time to accept just that.

CHAPTER TWENTY-SIX

THERE WAS A big event happening at the house later that night, and Elena had been banished to the basement. Leo had told her there would be several important guests in attendance and it was better if she stayed out of sight.

She didn't tell Leo how much that hurt her. She had been free for months, and she knew her place. She knew she wasn't to speak to anyone unless spoken to, knew that she was to do her work to perfection, but still, it wasn't good enough. They didn't want her in public where she might embarrass them.

No one spoke to her much. The other staff looked at her as if she were diseased, and she found herself lonely so much of the time, her only joy was when Leo came to see her, spoke kind words to her. But he'd been gone for days — some trip for the boss and she was lonelier than ever before.

She didn't feel like watching videos and she didn't want to read a book she'd already read. So she continued to wander the basement. She hadn't snooped through things before. Leo hadn't told her anything down in the basement was off limit, but she still hesitated as she began opening cupboards and looking through things.

It wasn't her place to look into what wasn't hers. That thought almost made her smile. Nothing was hers. She was often reminded of that, often told she was lucky to have a job at this prestigious house. Elena thought they must be right. Where would she be if they hadn't agreed to take her in when the master had died? She didn't want to even imagine the world outside of the protective walls harboring her.

No windows gave her light to see what was happening in the outside world, and the solitude of the basement made her feel as if she were going slightly stir crazy. She found a wooden box in the back of one of the cupboards and pulled it out.

Looking toward the hallway that led out of the basement, she felt her heart racing as she wondered if she was doing something wrong. Her fingers rubbed over the top of the box. Would she get in trouble if she opened it? Again, no one had told her anything in the basement was off limits.

Her fingers trembling, Elena lifted the lid, and found a leather bound book inside. Without knowing why, tears popped into her eyes as she reached inside and rubbed the cracked cover. There was something scratching at her memory as her fingers traced the picture of a dove etched into the leather.

She closed her eyes and that image of the little boy was there. It was blurry but she could almost see him sitting in front of her, his fingers tracing over a book. His laughter seemed to echo through the silent room.

"Who are you?" she said aloud, her voice quiet, almost spooky in the cold room.

His face turned up, but she couldn't see his features. It was all still a blur. But something inside her heart pounded as she tried to remember, as she tried to figure out the significance of this moment.

The videos of a family she'd often watched had told her she'd once had a family. Could this blonde boy be someone special to her? Or was it all in her head, a way for her to escape her own loneliness? Elena didn't know.

She pulled out the book at the bottom of the wooden box and carefully opened the cover. She saw writing there, faded blue ink appearing to be hastily scratched across the pages.

It wasn't a book, it was a journal.

"If you put your hand on that and close your eyes and think about me, you will know I'm out there, and I'm thinking about you." Those words echoed in the air around her and a shiver rushed through Elena's body.

Was this a memory breaking through her consciousness, or was she creating a story in her own head. Elena didn't know. She held the journal as if it were a lifeline to another world and tears streaked down her cheeks.

Her fingers felt scorched as she touched the pages, and she jerked her hand back, looking around again. Was this another dream? Was she truly in her bed, tossing and turning, about to wake up in a cold sweat? She pinched her arm and felt pain. She was very much awake.

She tried telling herself to scratch the wall would be a mistake, but she couldn't help herself from doing it. Even if it produced nothing but pain, wouldn't it be better for Elena to know who she was? Something deep within her, told her that she needed to tear that wall down.

So instead of putting the journal back, she slowly reached out and touched it again, this time setting it on her lap and opening it as she ran her fingers down the page. She was afraid to read what was written, but at the same time, she wondered if the words would answer some of her own questions, questions she didn't even know how to articulate.

I think I've been here for over a year. Not a day goes by that I don't pray for someone to save me, to take me back to my old life. They think I've been brainwashed, they think I know where my place is. But I remember it all. I remember my mom, my big sister. I remember playing softball at school, and laughing with my friends.

The master is a horrible man. He's hurt me in so many ways I can't even begin to describe them. He's taken not only my body, but my sprit as well. I don't think I will ever get out of this place, at least not alive, I won't. That's why I decided to write in this journal. They might find it and burn it. They probably will punish me again, or possibly kill me. I have fought this whole time to survive. I decided after the first month of torture that I would do whatever it took to go back home. But they've beaten out my will to even live.

I know I should end it, but I'm too afraid. My mom took me to church every Sunday and I remember my teacher saying that we couldn't get to heaven if we took our own life. So I've just prayed that God would save me, take me away from this — even if it's through death. So far my prayers haven't been answered. I still haven't given up on my faith. Even when the master does the most horrific things to me, I still believe.

It's the only thing I have left on this earth. It's been so long since I've been home and I'm sure my family thinks I'm dead. They probably searched for me for a while, but then they would have had to let go of me. My big sister would help them heal. They will all be okay.

I think I'm sixteen now. I'm not sure. I kept track of time passing in the beginning, but soon one day has faded into the next. There are no holidays, there is nothing here but pain and emptiness. I'll do what I can to make it through each day, but I fear none of it will be enough. I think I'll just eventually cease to exist ...

Elena was heartbroken as she read the words of the girl feeling so much pain while she wrote. There were smudges on the pages as she flipped through them. Elena ran her fingers over the spots, places where she was sure the girl's tears had dropped.

She continued reading, where the girl wrote in detail what the master had done to her. Elena's heart pounded with fear. That had almost been Elena's fate. If that had happened would she have been strong enough to write it all down? Would she have survived as long as the girl in the journal?

One day the entries stopped. Elena flipped through the empty pages, but nothing else was written on them. Did that mean the girl had died? Or had she been set free. There were places she spoke of them telling her if she did what she was supposed to she would be rewarded, she would earn her freedom. Elena wanted to believe it was true.

As she tucked the journal into the wooden box and slipped it back into place in the back of the cupboard, she wondered if she too would earn her freedom. She'd been scared when Dalton had told her he should set her free. She'd been afraid of what was out there beyond the walls of this property.

But as she read the journal, she thought she was a fool. This place might not be the sanctuary she thought it was. She might just be as much of a prisoner now as she'd been when they'd been prepping her for the master.

But even if they did allow Elena to go, she had no place to run to. This was the only home she could remember. The memories trying to break free in her mind only spoke of pain and suffering. Was that a world she wanted to be a part of?

Yes, it wasn't always perfect in this place she found herself in, but she was cared for, fed, and had a place to lay her head. If the world outside were as bad as Leo told her it was, she was a lot better off where she was.

And when the girl had written of her heartache in the journal, she'd been the master's toy. The master was now dead. Dalton was now the head of the house and he wasn't a monster. And of course she had Leo. Anything and anyone else, she could deal with.

No, Elena didn't need to leave. She was where she belonged and she would prove to them with her good behavior that she could be trusted. She wouldn't go snooping again in the basement. She didn't want to find any more clues of what this place had been, and she didn't want to tear the wall down. There was too much trauma that was sure to come with that.

Elena heard the door open and close at the top of the stairs and then she heard the creaks in the stairs as someone descended them. She guiltily looked at the cupboard she'd placed the journal back in, and let out a relieved sigh when she found that it was securely closed. No one would know what she had done. She told herself she was safe.

When Ken walked into the room, she was surprised. She couldn't ever remember him coming down to the basement. He looked around the room in disgust and then his eyes locked on hers, the same expression in them. She was as filthy as he deemed the room. Why it mattered to her what he thought, she would never understand.

"We have a staff member who suddenly came down with the flu. Your services are required," Ken told her in his uptight voice.

"What do you need me to do?" she asked, eager to make him happy.

"I don't think it's a good idea, but you will be picking up after the guests while they are having their function," he said.

"Picking up?" she asked. His eyes narrowed. He appeared to be annoyed she was asking for more of an explanation. But wouldn't it be better if she asked now and didn't mess up in front of the guests.

"People will set down plates, napkins, empty glasses and other items. You are to come behind them and clear the area. We don't want to appear unkempt now, do we?" he said, then looked at her as if she were the most unkempt thing on the property. He was probably right.

"Of course I can do that," she assured him.

"Go and shower. I'll send one of the maids down with your costume and she will get you ready," he told her. He then turned and walked from the room.

She wanted to ask him more questions, but she didn't dare do that. Instead, she waited for the door to close and then she jumped up and rushed to the bathroom to shower. She was going to finally get to be out while others were in the house. Even if she was nothing more than a servant, she could discreetly watch the people as they milled about the room.

Elena had never been as excited as she was in this moment. She couldn't quit smiling as she showered as quickly as possible. It was a party — and she was somewhat invited.

CHAPTER TWENTY-SEVEN

MUSIC PLAYED IN the background as more than a hundred guests moved through the large room in Dalton's place. Elena wore a mask over her eyes, as did the rest of the staff. A black silk dress clung to her body, the soft material stopping only a few inches from the bottom of her behind. Her legs were bare, and her feet ached from moving around the room in three-inch red stiletto heels.

Her and the rest of the staff were part of the decorations of the elaborate party. More than one man's fingers had skimmed her behind as she'd walked past. Her body was tense, but she had continued moving through the room, trying to ignore the crude comments thrown her way.

Elena knew she was nothing more than property, and the reason she'd been chosen to replace the other staff member was because she would look good in the outfit that had been chosen. Her painted red lips were to remain in a semblance of a smile, but she wasn't to make eye contact with any of the guests — which were mostly made of up males. And she wasn't to speak unless spoken to.

The few females in the room wore elegant dresses, their cleavage showed off to perfection, jewels dripping from their throats.

Dalton walked among the people in a black tux, clearly the lord and master of the room. All of the wealthy people were eager to please him. Elena found herself wanting to do the same.

No matter where she was in the room, she managed to follow him with her eyes. She hadn't been caught so far, and she was grateful for that. She'd been clearly told to keep her distance. Ken had warned her he didn't like the way she looked at the boss. He'd told her she was a fool if she thought she could catch the attention of a man as powerful as Dalton.

Elena *was* a fool. She was a nobody. But even knowing this, she still found herself gazing after the man, wondering what it would be like to have someone like him truly notice her.

Yes, there were many men in the room, sophisticated, good-looking men, who had most definitely noticed her with their slimy fingers touching her in any way they wanted. But none of them compared to Dalton.

The night continued, the men growing drunker as they sipped on fine champagne and ate delicate morsels of food that made Elena's stomach growl in hunger. As the night wore on, the men grew bolder in their touches, and she found herself fighting tears.

She'd wanted to attend the party — even as a servant, but she'd had no idea what it would be like. Ken watched over the staff, made sure they did their jobs correctly and when he got a chance he pulled her aside and admonished her for tempting the men.

Gaining a small amount of backbone, Elena let out a frustrated breath. "I am not the one who chose this outfit to display myself," she whispered harshly. "And you clearly told me not to speak to the guests. I can't help it if they are touching me."

Ken's eyes narrowed as his mouth twitched. She could see the rage in his eyes and she had no doubt that when he got her in private again she was going to pay for her outburst. Right now, it felt worth it. When his fist connected with her sensitive face, she might feel differently.

"Get to work. We will discuss this later," he threatened her. Elena decided she couldn't dwell on that. If she did, she wouldn't be able to keep her mask in place as she continued moving through the guests.

For a higher class of people, they were incredibly rude and sloppy. She'd even had one woman turn to find Elena nearby, and put her used napkin in the V of Elena's dress. If she thought she couldn't sink any lower, she was sure she'd be proven wrong.

Passing a man, he let his fingers slide across her chest, and Elena was so startled she met his gaze. He grabbed her arm and licked his lips as he leaned close to her. Elena didn't know what to do, but she knew she couldn't cause a scene.

"Hello there," he said in his slimy voice.

"Can I help you with something?" she asked, her voice weak in her fear.

"You could come somewhere a little more private with me," he suggested.

"I'm sorry, sir, I'm not allowed to go anywhere with the guests," she told him as she tried to pull from his grip. He didn't let her go.

"Aren't you supposed to attend to the needs of the guests here?" he said, his words an obvious threat. Elena didn't know what to do. If she somehow displeased Dalton, he would surely kick her from his home. But this man wasn't letting her go.

"Is there a problem here?"

Elena felt like weeping when she heard the harsh tone of Dalton standing right behind her. He moved up so she could see his face and he looked down at her with an unreadable expression in his eyes.

"I was suggesting to this young lady that we find somewhere much more private to … speak," the man said as he gave a wink to Dalton.

Dalton's expression didn't change as his gaze moved from hers to the man gripping her arm. He pointedly looked to where the man's fingers dug into her skin.

"I think you've had too much to drink, Roy. Let go of the woman before the two of us have a problem," Dalton told him.

His words came out quietly but there was most definitely a threat behind them. The authority in his tone was unmistakable. The man's fingers dropped instantly from her arm and Elena wanted to rub the skin, but refrained from doing so.

"You're excused," Dalton told her, his gaze briefly meeting hers.

She didn't stick around to hear the rest of Dalton's conversation with Roy, but moved swiftly away to the other side of the room. She wanted to leave the party, but she knew better than to do that, so she continued her work, continued to be inappropriately touched by men, and fought the tears wanting to fall.

Ken made sure to keep making eye contact with her, and there was promised retribution in his gaze. She hadn't done anything wrong, but she was quickly learning that it didn't matter if it was her fault or not. In Ken's eyes — hell, maybe in the world's eyes too — it would always be her fault.

It was two in the morning and it appeared as if the party was never going to end. The guests were still in high sprits and Elena's body ached as she moved as silently as possible around the room. She hadn't eaten in twelve hours, and she felt as if a light wind could blow her over. But the staff weren't even allowed to have breaks. The guests might need something, and it would be unacceptable to not be served, or cleaned up after, immediately.

At least the party began to calm as people went off to other areas for privacy or moved out to the terrace to smoke cigars and talk business. Elena looked across the room and didn't find a single item out of place, and decided it was a good moment to take three minutes to herself.

If she could get off her feet for just a few seconds, and possibly sneak in a couple bites of food, she was sure she would be in much better shape to serve at the party she wasn't sure would ever end.

She slipped through a door and moved swiftly in the direction of the kitchen. She didn't make it far before someone grabbed her arm and tugged her into a darkened room, then pushed her up against the wall.

A scream got caught in Elena's throat as fear spiked through her. She barely managed to hold the sound back. But if she let it out, it didn't matter what was about to happen to her, the punishment would be even worse.

"Are you trying to sneak off, Elena?" Dalton asked, his voice low and calm.

Her fear instantly disappeared as butterflies took over in her stomach. Dalton's body pushed up against hers as he pressed her harder into the wall. She looked up at him, immediately lost in his intense gaze.

"No, sir. I was just … running to the bathroom," she said, thinking as fast on her feet as she could with her nerves scattered.

"Hmm," he said, the sound rumbling through his chest. "I can't seem to take my eyes off you tonight."

Those words came out with anger. Elena just didn't know why he was mad at her. She'd been keeping her head down. Sure, she had looked at him quite often, but he hadn't caught her doing it — or she hadn't thought he had.

"I'm sorry," she said, not knowing what else to say.

"I don't think you are," he said.

He lifted a hand and gripped the back of her neck. Elena looked at his tight expression and the hard line of his lips. She couldn't say anything to him. There was no way she was going to argue.

"No. I don't think you're sorry at all. I think you like me looking at you," he said. His mouth was so close to hers, every word he spoke caused his warm breath to cascade over her.

Elena felt that stirring deep inside her again, felt wet heat rush through her. She couldn't even begin to comprehend what he was doing to her.

"I'm trying to stay out of the way," she told him.

"You're everywhere," he said, the words an accusation. "I can't turn around without you in my face."

"I'll try to do better," she promised.

He growled low in his throat and then closed the small distance between them, his lips crashing against hers in a brutal kiss. Elena's arms were pinned between their bodies, but even if they hadn't been, she wouldn't fight him. She wasn't sure what she wanted, but she didn't have the will to pull away from this man.

His tongue pushed past the barrier of her lips and she gasped into his mouth as he pressed against her, molding her to him.

Reaching down, his fingers gripped the back of her thigh and he raised her leg, thrusting his hips forward, pressing his hardness against her center.

The ache she felt around him intensified as he devoured her mouth and his fingers dug into her thigh. A moan escaped her lips, and she got lost in him as he held her in place while masterfully working her mouth and body.

After several moments Dalton wrenched his face from hers, and Elena's eyes slowly opened as she gazed at him in surprise. She was shaking against him as she stared into his molten eyes. He narrowed his gaze before releasing her leg and taking a small step back.

"What in the fuck are you doing to me?" he growled as his fingers reached up and he gripped her chin harshly. She shook beneath his touch, but didn't dare try to move. She also didn't try to answer him.

He breathed heavily as the two of them remained locked in the others gaze for several tense moments. She couldn't even begin to imagine what he was thinking as he stared at her.

"I shouldn't have done this. It's so damn wrong," he said. He released his grip on her and stepped back, no longer touching her.

Elena felt emptiness where he'd been pressed against her, and she found herself wanting to reach for him. She had no one to help her understand what she was feeling and she had to fight the urge to touch him, to ask for his forgiveness, though she wasn't sure what she'd done wrong.

"Go get yourself cleaned up and get back out there," he told her.

Dalton straightened his clothes, then he turned around and walked from the room. Elena stood there a couple moments as she got her breathing back under control. Then she made her way to the bathroom, shocked when she saw her flushed cheeks and messy hair.

It took her too long to put herself back together, but when she was finished she hoped no one would notice. She'd been gone a while and she was sure Ken would notice that for sure. If he knew why she'd been gone, she knew it would ensure the man's wrath.

Elena snuck back into the main room and kept her face turned down, looking only at the surfaces of tables and chairs, not meeting anyone's eyes. That's why she didn't see the lethal stare Ken gave her — or notice that Leo was back, and he was figuring out exactly what was going on, even if she wasn't.

CHAPTER TWENTY-EIGHT

"HAPPY BIRTHDAY, ELENA."

Leo handed her a sugar cookie with frosting on it, and she glanced at him in surprise.

"I can't remember if it's my birthday or not," she finally said.

"I don't know your *actual* birthday, but it's how long you've been here," he said. "You're nineteen."

"How long *have* I been here?" Time had no meaning.

"A little over two years," he told her. "But it looks like things won't be so bad anymore. Ken has been fired, and the boss said that if any of the staff lay a single finger on another member, they will be escorted off the premises." He was quiet a moment. "I somehow think you had something to do with that."

"I didn't say anything," she quickly defended.

"I'm sure you didn't." He was quiet again as he looked to the ground and then back up. What was in his eyes was different from anything she'd seen before. "I'm sorry for all you've gone through, and the part I've played in it."

Elena was in shock as Leo stood before her, shifting from foot to foot. This was the one man who had never been particularly cruel to her. He'd had to do his job, though, and sometimes that included punishment.

She definitely felt a strong connection with him. She also knew it was because she didn't have anyone else, and he had almost always been kind to her. It was easy to be with him.

"I'm fine, Leo," she finally whispered.

He took a step closer. "The rules are that there's to be no more abuse. The boss hasn't said anything about the staff not being allowed to . . . date," he finally said.

"What are you talking about, Leo?" She was suddenly nervous.

"You've grown up, Elena," he responded.

He moved even closer, and then he was cupping the back of her head. Elena panicked. She didn't want to make this man mad, one of the few men who had been kind to her, but she also didn't want him to touch her like this.

"What are you doing?" she asked, trying to step back.

"Don't fight this, Elena." His tone changed, became more frightening as he grabbed her and pulled her against him.

"Leo . . ." Her voice was barely more than a whimper.

"I never thought I would want you, care about you. I never have with any of the girls. But normally they're gone by now. You've just been so . . . strong. You've grown into such a beautiful woman. I know you feel the connection too. I know it's more than friendship," he said, his voice a little crazy. This was a side of Leo she hadn't experienced before and it was scaring her badly.

He grabbed her behind, pulling her tightly against him. She struggled against the hold, trying to push away. This wasn't what she wanted. This wasn't a comforting touch like he normally used with her.

"Stop!" he thundered. She went still. "That's better. It's better if you don't fight, Elena."

The look in his eyes was almost wild. Where had the normally kind man gone? Who was this person?

"I've wanted you for a long time. I'm in love with you, Elena." There was something almost feral about the way he was looking at her, the way he was speaking.

She didn't recognize the man she'd come to look at as her savior in so many ways. And his touch wasn't the same as Dalton's. He didn't make butterflies appear in her stomach or make her want to lean into him. She wanted nothing more than to pull away from him.

"I don't even know what love it," she whimpered as he leaned in and ran his tongue along her neck.

She felt none of the same feelings she'd felt when Dalton had virtually done the same thing. Maybe it was because somehow she had known she'd had a choice that night with Dalton. Right now, she knew she had no say in what was happening. That had to be the difference. She wasn't sure, but she tried to reason with Leo again.

"You've been good to me, Leo. I appreciate all you've done for me and more than that, I appreciate our friendship, but I've been touched so much, I've been hurt . . ." she tried to explain.

He either wasn't capable of hearing her in this moment, or he thought he was entitled. Whatever it was, he didn't pull away, and her fear grew. He bent down and his lips covered hers. Silently, she wept as he crushed his body against hers, and his tongue plundered her mouth.

He pulled back and looked at her again. "Haven't I been good to you?" he demanded.

Elena shook in his arms. This wasn't the comforting touch of a friend. This was one more man taking from her what he could because he was stronger. She'd thought Leo was her friend. That's what was making this so much worse. She'd never expected this from him.

"I asked you a question," he said, his voice growing more agitated.

"You have been my friend, Leo. Please don't do this?" she begged.

He looked furious at her words. She knew to fight him any longer would do her no good. She'd been wrong about Leo, so wrong. She wasn't sure what was breaking her heart more — the violation against her body, or the betrayal of the only friend she had.

"You will like this, you'll see. You're just scared," he told her. She just wasn't sure if he was trying to convince her or himself.

He began stripping her, as he'd done so many times before. But now, it was different. She knew it was different. When she was naked and he laid her on the bed, she wept.

"It's not that bad, Elena. It would have been so much worse for you long ago with the master. It's not that bad," Leo kept saying over and over again.

He paused as he looked into her eyes with an almost maniacal expression. He was trying to get her to agree with him. She could see that, but she couldn't tell him she wanted this. It was nothing she wanted.

She turned her head away and stared at the wall, crying out as pain shot through her. He still didn't stop.

The men had degraded her, had swept their fingers inside her, had slapped her all over, but no one had committed sex with her before. That was to be saved for the master. The pain was excruciating as he thrust himself in her and moved up and down. She could barely breathe through the nausea and despair as one more thing was stolen from her.

When he was finished, he stood above her.

"See. It wasn't so bad," he said. She knew he wanted her to say something, but she couldn't speak. Her body shivered as he threw a blanket over her. "It wasn't so bad. It will get better."

His fingers trailed through her hair and wiped at her tears. She wasn't sure if he was trying to convince her or himself. Finally, she mustered the strength to turn away from him and face the wall, lying there in the fetal position as she sobbed.

Why she should even care, she wasn't sure, but she did care. She hurt, and she was defeated, more defeated than she'd ever felt since remembering this life. She'd been told this was her entire purpose, to please a man. This was what she was trained to do. She'd been molded to please the master. But then the master had died, and she'd found a bit of freedom.

That freedom had just painfully ended.

CHAPTER TWENTY-NINE

OVER THE NEXT month, Elena didn't even try to fight off Leo when he would visit her. When she fought him, he became rougher, made the experience so much worse. He always told her it would get better.

The pain stopped, but she always went to the shower after, scrubbed her body until she nearly bled, and huddled in a ball on her bed, still feeling dirty, still feeling out of control. How did anyone survive a life like this?

If these people had found her, had brought her into their home to save her, then shouldn't they want to take care of her, not abuse her? She was so confused.

There was nowhere for her to hide, though. Ken was gone and a new, stern woman was in his place. The woman wasn't kind, however she didn't use violence to get her way. She simply used slashing words. But she didn't hate Elena. She didn't praise her; then again she never made Elena go over something she'd already cleaned before.

That was a small blessing in her otherwise bleak life.

She saw Dalton a few more times — from a distance. He didn't speak to her again, and she shouldn't hope he would, but she looked for him when she was in the house or when she was in the yard.

She assured herself she was only doing this out of curiosity. She had no interest in him. It would do her no good if she did. He was everything she wasn't — sophisticated, respected, needed. Free.

She wasn't sure what the kisses and touching had been about, but the more time she had to think about it, the more she realized he'd just slipped up. He'd seen her there, knew what her purpose was — to please a man — and decided to test her out — twice.

She hadn't passed the tests.

She was grateful for that, she told herself. Because even though he'd sparked something inside her when he'd pulled her onto his lap, the tangible act of sex was rough and dissatisfying. She dreaded when Leo would climb on top of her.

He asked her each time if she'd enjoyed herself, and after enduring his wrath when she hadn't answered him right, she'd learned to tell him she had. That would calm him down. He kept telling her he did it because he loved her.

Elena didn't understand love, had no comprehension of it. But if love, something she read about in the books she took to her small room, was what Leo was showing her, then she wanted no part of it.

Maybe it was because of her time with Leo that she was so fascinated with Dalton. The more she was away from him, the more she put him on a pedestal. Somehow in all the chaos of her world, he was the anchor in her storm, what Leo used to be. Although Dalton had barely spoken more than a few dozen words to her, when she did spot him from a distance, it grounded her.

Walking outside in the garden, she heard a voice, turned from her favorite secluded area, and saw him pacing in the distance, his phone held up to his ear as he snapped words to whoever he was speaking to.

Without even thinking about it, she lifted her hand and touched her lips where he'd made her feel unimaginable things.

She slunk down and peered at him from the bushes, not wanting him to know she was there. She rarely had the opportunity to gaze at him for any length of time, and without him knowing she was there, she could look as long as she wanted.

As she stared, he continued speaking, his voice irritated. He wore a fitted white shirt, and as he spoke and paced, he reached a hand up to yank on his tie, the red splash of material instantly loosening as it fell open, hanging from his neck.

"I don't give a damn about the cost. Get it done," he said, his voice rising before he hung up and pushed the phone into his pants pocket.

Suddenly his head whipped around, and their eyes connected from across the yard. Elena froze as she tried to slink down farther. Even though she was hidden, she had no doubt he'd spotted her. His eyes didn't release hers as he began moving in her direction.

She thought for a moment about running. But it was already too late. It would be best to just face the music. She stepped from behind the shrubs, cursing the small opening that she'd been peeking through.

"I'm so sorry. I didn't mean to listen. I was walking and then you were here and—"

"Silence!" he snapped. She shut up immediately.

He moved steadily and quickly approached, grabbing her arm and yanking her around to the side of the garden and farther away from the main house. Elena wasn't sure what was going to happen next.

When they were in a secluded area of the yard, a place she hadn't been before, he pushed her back, her body trapped against the side of a large shed.

"You just seem to keep popping up all over the place, don't you?" he growled.

She wasn't sure how he meant the words — if he wanted her to answer them, explain herself, or if she was still supposed to be silent. Her throat burned with unsaid explanations. Why hadn't she just turned around?

"You might be a curse I have to deal with," he continued, and his eyes narrowed.

She still didn't speak. Her knees shook, and she was frightened. But she also didn't want him to leave her there all alone, or worse yet, leave her for Leo to find.

He stepped closer to her, and his fingers began running through her hair. He let the strands slide between his fingers as he gazed at her. She was mesmerized.

"Don't say a word," he warned.

The same butterflies she'd felt the first time he'd looked at her this way rose in her stomach, and she tilted her head the slightest bit for easier access. At least she now knew how to respond to a man. Would he be able to tell the difference?

As Dalton's lips connected with hers, the butterflies exploded, the feeling so much more intense than the last time. She found she wanted to wrap her arms around his neck, wanted to hold on to him, wanted to do more than just kiss him. Maybe sex wasn't such a bad thing. Maybe Leo just wasn't good at it.

Maybe it was all about choice.

She fisted her fingers at her sides in an effort not to grab him. He'd told her to be still. She wasn't sure how she was supposed to react to this suave man kissing her again. But as his lips coaxed hers to open, she did so willingly, and hoped it wouldn't end too quickly.

He gripped her hair tightly as he deepened the kiss, his mouth firm and controlling, while also eliciting a response from her. When he leaned back, his eyes were blazing with passion and anger.

He pushed his hips forward, and she had no doubt she was feeling his arousal. What made her unsure was how she was reacting to it. She wanted him to do the things Leo had done to her. What was the matter with her?

He leaned back into her and then lifted her leg up as he pushed forward even harder, his thickness resting right against her throbbing core. She groaned into his mouth, which seemed to make him go a bit mad.

His hand descended from her hair and slid down her throat, gliding over the top of her shirt until he was squeezing her breast. She groaned again as his palm rubbed her erect nipple through the thin cotton. She squirmed against him, wanting to be closer.

When his hand lowered, she wanted to complain until it slid beneath her shirt and traveled upward once again, quickly unclasping her bra and then cupping her sensitive flesh before he squeezed the nipple between two fingers.

Heat unlike anything she could imagine flooded her insides as wetness coated her core, begging this man to finish what he'd started.

Her hands were clasped behind his neck without her having any idea how they'd gotten there. But that seemed to be the only thing anchoring her to the massive wall of his body.

When he pulled back, fire blazed in his eyes, and he squeezed her tender flesh one more time. She panted and hung on to him. When he let go of her breast, she whimpered, and his eyes narrowed before reaching behind his neck and unclasping her hands, firmly setting them back at her sides before he took a step back.

"Yes, you are a curse," he said.

He moved back farther and sent her a withering look before he turned and strode away. Elena leaned against the wall and fought the emotions — the feelings — that were rushing through her.

That shouldn't have happened. She never should have stayed and watched him when she realized he was in the yard. She should have slithered back into the shed — into her hiding place.

But it *had* happened, and she couldn't undo it.

Her fingers pressed against her lips, her body trembling. Finally, she redid her bra and dragged herself to her basement. Even later, lying in bed and smiling, she knew there was a problem.

That night she dreamed of Dalton; she dreamed of being his.

And when Leo came to her later and forced himself upon her, she closed her eyes and pictured it being Dalton above her; Dalton kissing her. She imagined it was just the two of them on a deserted island where no one was cruel to her, no one took anything from her, only gave her pleasure.

And, although at the end of it she still felt filthy and needed to clean herself of Leo's smell, it wasn't quite as painful. It was almost bearable.

With an imagination, she just might survive this place, survive Leo.

CHAPTER THIRTY

THE WARM AIR didn't have so much as a breeze stirring it as Elena enjoyed her favorite spot in the garden among the shrubs and trees, away from prying eyes — away from Leo and his constant unwanted lust.

The shadows were where she belonged. Among them she could hide away, living almost in a new reality. She loved the shadows, loved the darkness, especially when there was light just beyond them. Light she could see into, but darkness where she dwelled, where she couldn't be seen.

She heard the voices, alerting her she was no longer alone, before she saw a couple moving slowly to the gazebo, a dozen yards from where she was hidden away. Glancing around her, she made sure she was still shrouded in the shadows, and once she felt safe, she slunk back the slightest bit to be sure.

They would soon go away, and she could resume her thoughts in the dark. The last time she'd spied on Dalton, it had led to the kiss . . . and more. Of course, that didn't make her want to run away, that made her want to be caught.

As much as she didn't want to look, Elena couldn't help but stare as Dalton leaned against the gazebo railing, his attention focused on a brunette with long hair cascading down her back, and a dress so short and tight Elena wondered if she had difficulty sitting.

She didn't look at the woman long though. It was too difficult to pull her gaze away from the man with his piercing brown eyes she was unable to see from her position. It didn't matter if she could see his eyes or not. Looking into them one time was all it took to remember them in her dreams forever.

He wasn't smiling as he gazed at the woman, simply watching her as she chattered away. His arms were crossed in front of him, one foot casually placed over the other as the banister supported his weight.

Elena could hear every word the woman was saying, though it wasn't anything worth remembering. Something about a fashion show and how excited she was to travel to Paris in a month. Elena had no clue what a fashion show was.

Dalton said something, but Elena couldn't quite pick up the words, his voice was so low. But the woman must have delighted in whatever it was, because her neck went back and she laughed. She took a step closer to him and placed her perfectly manicured hands on his chest, her lips inching ever closer to his.

He still didn't shift his position. He looked almost . . . bored.

But that certainly couldn't be. Not when he was with a woman whose body was perfect, whose laughter sounded like music, and who would most likely know exactly how to please a man like him.

Not that Elena would know precisely what he'd like. She didn't know what anyone liked except Leo. That thought sent a shudder through her. But she had felt Dalton's hardness between her thighs, so she thought he liked sex.

The woman must have noticed she didn't have his full attention, because she licked her lips and leaned against him, finally making him uncross his arms. He moved his hands to her hips as she pushed forward, connecting their mouths.

Elena knew she should leave. She was invading Dalton's privacy, and if he found out, he'd be furious. But she *couldn't* leave. She was trapped right where she was, gazing at the couple, as the kiss grew more heated.

The woman pulled back, a moan echoing across the yard as she reached low and rubbed Dalton between his legs.

He seemed to enjoy that more than anything else that had happened so far. He pulled her face back to his and devoured her mouth, one hand fisting in her hair and holding her in place while the other gripped her ass and tugged her closer.

When he released her lips, he pulled on her hair, making her head fall back, and he trailed his lips down her neck and into the ample cleavage of her dress before moving over the tight material where he did something that made the woman yelp.

That brought a smile to his lips.

"Let's go inside, Dalton," she purred.

"No. Right here," he told her.

She seemed unsure for a moment as she looked around. She looked right to the place where Elena was hiding, but her gaze continued on. There was no way either of them could see her.

Dalton didn't bother looking around. He obviously didn't care if they had privacy or not. In fact he seemed excited by the prospect of having sex with an audience. Not that he could possibly know Elena was watching. She slunk back just a bit more to be sure, but her eyes were glued to the couple.

The woman reached behind her and unzipped her dress, letting the strapless top fall down, revealing her perky, naked breasts. Dalton reached for them, his hands holding their weight as his thumbs rubbed over the nipples, making the woman cry out in pleasure.

Elena couldn't tear her gaze away as the couple went back to kissing, Dalton's hands all over her as he lifted the bottom of her dress up, then gripped her nearly bare ass in his palms.

"On your knees," he told the woman.

Elena was shocked to see the woman immediately drop. She didn't even hesitate as she began undoing his pants. He gripped her hair as she pulled him from his pants and licked the tip of his hardness.

Dalton was positioned perfectly, giving Elena an unspoiled view of his entire body. As the woman held his thickness in her hand, it overflowed, a solid, perfect rod of steel. She didn't know they could be that . . . big . . . or thick. Leo wasn't even close to looking like Dalton when he was excited.

She couldn't tear her gaze away as the woman took him in her mouth, making his head roll back as he moaned his approval while her cherry lips took him deeper and deeper down her throat.

Then Dalton's fingers fastened even tighter into the woman's hair, and he held her still as he began pumping his hips, moving at the speed he wanted. The woman choked a bit and he growled at her. She stopped immediately.

Faster and faster, he moved against the woman's tongue, his thickness expanding her throat, making him groan in pleasure. Saliva dripped from her lips as she held on to his hips and tried to keep steady.

Leo had forced Elena to do this on him, but he'd never been so rough with her while doing it. Maybe she should be grateful he wasn't hurting her — or hadn't physically hurt her since that night he'd taken her for the first time. Sure he was rough, but he never shoved his thickness down her throat to where she couldn't breathe.

Elena should have been horrified watching this scene play out in front of her, should have been disgusted at the sounds Dalton was making, the slight choking from the woman on her knees with her breasts swaying from the force of Dalton's thrusts.

But she wasn't.

She was wet with hunger, watching this go on. She wanted to *be* that woman.

The thought horrified her so much that a soft gasp escaped her lips.

She threw a hand over her mouth and stared at the couple. There was no way they had heard her. Not with the noise they were making. It had barely been a whisper of a breath.

But still, Dalton's head turned, and he looked right where Elena was sitting on the ground while he continued thrusting his arousal into the woman's mouth. Elena didn't move so much as a finger as she sat there in the bushes, his gaze seeming to bore into her.

He couldn't see her. She knew that. It was all in her head that he could. She was in the shadows. She was safe in the shadows. Still, she didn't even breathe, only allowed a slight trickle of air in and out, making sure her chest wasn't even moving.

He finally turned away and pulled his shining arousal from the woman's mouth. Her lips were swollen, and she wiped the spit from her chin as he leaned down and lifted her. She leaned in for a kiss, but he deflected it, quickly moving from where he'd been leaning against the side of the gazebo to a new spot that was even closer to Elena.

He pushed the woman's stomach against the railing and then bent her forward so her ass was sticking high in the air. With a quick tug of his fingers, he tore away the miniscule panties she was wearing and reached into his pocket and pulled out a packet, sliding latex onto his thick manhood.

They were both facing Elena now, who still didn't dare move. The woman was looking at the ground, her mouth forming a perfect O of satisfaction when Dalton slammed inside her body.

"Yes, Dalton, yes!" the woman screamed as he pounded against her, holding her hips tightly in his grasp. Lifting a hand, he slapped her skin, the sound echoing off the walls of the buildings on the property, making Elena flinch.

"Yes, baby, more," the woman told him, and he slapped her again.

"Finger yourself. I want you to squeeze every ounce of come from me," he demanded.

His voice was so hard, so controlled, although the faster he went a slight sheen of sweat began coating his forehead.

Elena couldn't look away from the couple.

And then his eyes found hers. She knew it wasn't possible, knew he couldn't see her, but his eyes were right on hers, their gazes locked together. She couldn't have turned away if there had been a gun to her head. She was mesmerized. Her body was dripping with unfulfilled desire.

"Touch yourself," he said again, this time his voice gentler, his eyes not budging.

He wasn't speaking to her, she assured herself.

But without realizing what she was doing, she reached down, trying to relieve the ache, doing exactly what he'd commanded she do, whether it was for her or the woman he was fucking. She didn't know how, didn't know what she was doing.

Leo was her only lover, and he was only worried about his satisfaction. She didn't even know she could feel anything like she was feeling right now. Her eyes locked on Dalton's, her hand was down her shorts, and she kept her gaze on his and moved her fingers.

Unbelievable pleasure built in her stomach. It was unlike anything she had ever imagined.

"Do you feel the heat?" Dalton asked.

Elena almost answered him, but the woman he was pounding against moaned and reminded Elena of her presence. But yes, Elena felt the heat, felt something she'd never imagined was possible to feel.

He slowed his thrusts, as his gaze seemed to bore right into Elena. Her core was slick and hot and her fingers found a place that made her want to scream out in pleasure. She focused on that place, a feeling of pressure building higher and higher, making her fingers swirl faster and faster.

As if he could feel her arousal through the air, he quickened his movements again, groans rushing through the air.

"Come now," Dalton demanded.

"Yes," the woman he was with screamed.

For an almost endless moment Elena had forgotten the woman was even there. But it didn't matter.

Elena's thighs were quivering, her stomach growing tighter and tighter, and tingles were rushing through her limbs, making her lightheaded. A sheen of sweat was coating her body as she desperately tried not to pant. Air was rushing quickly in and out of her nose, and she bit her lip so hard she tasted blood. But she couldn't stop. She couldn't look away from Dalton.

"Now, come now!" The command drifted through the air.

She flicked her finger over her tender place one more time and an explosion happened through her body. The tingles that had been there felt like nothing compared to what she was feeling now.

Somehow her eyes remained open as she shook violently. Though her vision blurred and she felt close to passing out, everything within her body lifted her to a previously unimaginable place. Dalton let out a growl of pleasure as the other woman screamed.

She shook in front of him and Dalton tensed, his eyes never leaving the place where Elena was now slumping in complete stupefaction. Her bones were jelly, her muscles most likely incapable of ever working again.

It was like he knew what had happened to her.

But he couldn't possibly know. His words had been for the woman he was with.

"That was insane, baby," the woman said as he pulled from her, took a step back while removing the condom, and began re-buttoning his pants.

"Yes, it was," he murmured. But he wasn't looking at the woman. He was still gazing into the bushes where Elena lurked, shaking.

He didn't say another word, just left the woman standing there, almost completely naked as he began moving toward the bushes.

Elena held her breath, terrified it hadn't been her imagination, terrified he knew she was there, and had known what she'd been doing. A smirk lifted his lips as he got closer.

He paused when he neared the bushes, but then his steps picked up, and he kept on walking. The woman in the gazebo yelled out after him, but he didn't slow his pace. Soon, he was out of sight.

Elena looked back over to the woman who was furiously putting her clothes — minus the destroyed panties — back into place. She then stomped away from the gazebo, presumably to chase after Dalton.

Elena stayed right where she was for a very long time. She didn't trust her muscles to work right. She also couldn't stand the thought of Leo coming to her room tonight and ruining this magical moment for her.

She napped on and off for hours, until just before dawn. Then she crept inside to the shower, avoiding her bed.

The cold new master of the house was all she could think about after this night. It was no longer a choice for her. She desired him even though she knew little of desire. And what was worse, she wanted him to want her.

Unlike his father, who she'd been primed for, she *wanted* to belong to this man. He'd awakened something inside of her, and she knew for sure she didn't want to put it back to sleep.

Elena just wasn't sure what that meant — what any of it meant.

CHAPTER THIRTY-ONE

"WHERE WERE YOU last night?"

The low threat in Leo's voice sent a chill down Elena's spine. She'd managed to avoid him the entire day, doing her chores and staying in the house, but night had fallen and she had to shower. She'd been cleaning beneath the furniture and felt grimy even though the house was always spotless.

"I fell asleep outside," she told him, holding the towel wrapped around her a little tighter.

"Are you sure you weren't off somewhere fucking the boss of the house?" he growled, taking a menacing step toward her.

How could he possibly know what she'd witnessed? He couldn't. She was so worried about the entire situation she was assuming things.

"No. Of course not," she finally gasped, her breathing accelerating in her fear. "Why would you even think that? The man has barely spoken more than a few words to me." Never before had she seen Leo so angry. "Have I done something to upset you?" she finally asked.

"Your presence has been requested by Dalton. I want to know why," he said, his eyes flashing rage.

"I don't know, Leo. Honestly I don't know. I've barely spoken to the man. I promise you," she said, taking a step back, making his eyes ignite even more. She certainly wasn't going to tell him about the kisses the two of them had shared or the scene in the garden.

"Don't move away from me," he roared. She stopped where she stood.

Quicker than a snake striking, his hand came up and gripped her hair, tugging it hard, making her cry out.

"You're mine, Elena. You won't forget that," he said before smashing his mouth against hers at the same time that he ripped the towel from her body.

She couldn't even respond as he painfully handled her. She fought the tears as he pushed her against the wall and proved she was his, whether she wanted to be or not.

When he was finished, rage was still shining in his eyes but he wasn't gripping her quite so tightly. She could feel bruises from his anger forming on her skin. She stood there shivering while he looked her over and shook his head.

"You won't tell Dalton about our relationship. Do you understand?" he snapped.

"Yes, I understand." It wouldn't do her any good to say anything anyway.

"You are mine, no matter what that piece of shit thinks."

He finally moved away and began pacing the floor in front of her. She didn't know if she was allowed to move, so she crossed her arms and leaned against the wall, grateful it was there to hold her up.

Leo moved toward her and examined her skin. "Dammit!" he snarled as he spun her around. "If he does bed you and asks about the bruises, you say the new gardener has been rough with you."

"Yes, Leo," she replied.

"Good. Go and take a shower. It's time to get you ready to see the boss. Don't be a slut," he snapped.

She turned and began to move back toward the bathroom when his hand shot out and hit her so hard on the behind she knew there would be another bruise there. The hit almost knocked her down, but she managed to catch herself.

Her tears didn't fall until she was beneath the shower spray. She leaned against the wall and sobbed, not understanding how her life had turned out this way — not comprehending how anyone could be so cruel.

Leo had once been the person she'd run to when the rest of the world seemed unstable. Now he was the biggest monster of them all. If only she could remember her past, then maybe she could escape.

But did she still want to escape? Especially after Dalton seemed to be taking an interest in her. Was her curiosity about Dalton worth Leo's wrath? She didn't have those answers for herself.

She knew not to take too long in the shower. She didn't want to endure more of Leo's anger. So she washed his scent away, scrubbed her skin hard, stepped out, and dried.

She knew better than to wrap the towel around her. It would only anger him that she was hiding from him. He enjoyed prepping her — enjoyed controlling her.

She hated him enough that she thought she might be capable of murder.

That was a sobering thought, one she hoped to never have again.

Leo was waiting for her in the sitting room, exactly where he'd been that first time he'd prepped her for the master of the house. This time, though, his manner was different. This time he was angry, and his eyes possessively roamed over her.

She stood in front of him as he examined her.

"You're not as bruised as I thought. That's good," he said. "Turn." She obeyed. "Very good."

He picked up the lotion and began rubbing it into her skin, taking extra time on her breasts, painfully pinching her nipples before moving to her backside and then slipping his fingers inside her until she had to fight yelping.

"Remember *who* you belong to," he said again.

"I won't forget, Leo," she told him. She was so afraid of breaking down she could barely speak.

Elena desperately wanted this night to end. She didn't know how much more she was capable of taking before she broke apart.

Leo finished with the lotion then pulled out a dress she'd never seen before.

"The boss sent this down," he said, not at all pleased about it.

It wasn't a particularly revealing dress, but the blue material was the softest she'd ever felt. After her miniscule bra and panties were in place, Leo slipped the dress over her head then turned her around to zip it; she almost smiled at how good it felt on her skin.

"I like this," she murmured without thinking.

The quick sting on her face warned her she'd said the wrong thing once again. She looked at Leo, not understanding.

"Don't get used to this high-end crap, Elena. Most people can't afford it," he snapped.

"I'm sorry. I didn't know," she said, rapidly blinking her eyes.

"Maybe you should just learn to keep your damn mouth shut before I stuff something in it to keep words from spewing out."

She decided that was the best advice she'd ever been given.

He glared at her for several moments before he reached down and began rubbing himself through his pants. She wanted to cry again when she saw the evidence of his arousal. He was angry, but seeing the pain he was causing her was exciting him all over again.

"On your knees," he snapped.

"But …" She couldn't even finish the words.

"I said on your knees," he thundered, reaching out and pinching her waist as he pushed her down.

She crumpled before him and her throat closed with unshed tears while he undid his pants and pulled out his hardness. He stroked it a few times before tilting her chin up, the angry light in his eyes boring into her.

Without another word, he gripped the back of her neck and pulled her forward. She wanted to pull back, but knew it would only end in trouble for her. Trying not to gag, she opened her mouth as he thrust himself into it then grabbed her on either side of her head and began thrusting his hips.

This was different than other times he'd made her do this. He was angry and uncontrolled, and he pushed himself deeper, making her gag, which pissed him off more if the yanking on her head was any indication.

"Take it all, bitch, and remember you belong to me," he growled. His voice was chocked with arousal as he pulled on her head, making her suck him faster.

"Tighten your lips," he groaned, and she did her best to comply. His hand unwrapped from around her hair and she felt the sting of his slap, making her see stars. "Stop biting me!"

Opening her jaw more, she prayed this would soon end.

He pushed in and out of her mouth while grunting and then the taste of his release slithering down her throat made her stomach turn, but with more willpower than she knew she was capable of, she managed not to heave.

She didn't pull from him though, knowing that would only cause more anger. She waited, and when his final shudders died away, he pulled his softening member from her sore mouth.

"You need to improve," he grumbled as he tucked himself away and jerked her upright. She stood before him, unable to know how she wasn't visibly trembling.

Elena knew better than to say anything else though, as he continued getting her ready to meet with Dalton. He wiped her mouth, powdered her cheek to cover the red and then gave her a final inspection before saying it was time to go.

"I should take you out of here now, just run away, the two of us," he said with a crazy look in his eyes.

She held her breath in terror. The thought of being alone with Leo would be a fate she couldn't imagine. It would be the ultimate form of torture. But she schooled her fears.

"I would like that, Leo," she said, hoping there was no way he'd be able to accomplish it. At one time, she would have loved slipping away with Leo. Not anymore.

"We'd never make it. There are gates, and the guards watch this place," he said. She could see him trying to wrack his brain to figure out a way to accomplish the task. Soon he gave up.

"Remember who owns you," he whispered at the top of the basement stairs, and then the talking stopped completely as they opened the door and crept into the shed before going through another door to the yard.

They quickly passed through the employee entrance to the house and then he moved through the rooms with her right behind him. When they ascended the main staircase, her stomach twisted. This was so much like the first walk she'd been taken on not that long ago, and she couldn't help but feel anxious.

But this time she wasn't on display for everyone in the house to see. This time she wouldn't be tied down to a bed — or at least she didn't think so. This time, she anxiously anticipated the moment when the door would open and she would see Dalton again.

She looked down, afraid that Leo would turn and be able to read those very thoughts in her eyes. She didn't think he'd dare hit her out in the open, but the retaliation could come later.

He stopped at a door and knocked, and Elena continued to look at the ground. When the door opened, she focused on the feet in front of her.

"Thank you, Leo. You're dismissed."

"Yes, Sir. What time would you like me to come back?" Leo said, his voice normal as he talked to his boss.

"I'll take her back. Go to bed."

Elena could imagine the fury that statement sent through Leo. She would bet he would be waiting — watching, wanting to know everything that happened. She didn't dare look in either man's direction. Leo turned and left, and she stood there not knowing what to do.

For once though she didn't want to run away — no, for once, she wanted to move forward and maybe plot out a new future for herself.

CHAPTER THIRTY-TWO

"COME INSIDE, ELENA. Dinner will be here shortly."

She moved forward without looking at Dalton. When she entered the room, she was pleasantly surprised. She'd been expecting a bedroom, but this was a sitting area with an elegant table and two chairs.

"Do you like the dress?"

He stood before her, his gaze examining the dress from her neck to her thighs where it rested.

"Yes, it's very comfortable," she whispered.

"The color matches your eyes. I knew you would look stunning in it."

She didn't know how to respond so she only murmured a quiet thank you.

"Sit down."

She moved to the table and waited to see which place she was supposed to sit. He held out one of the chairs and she took a seat, all without having even peeked at him.

He moved across the table and sat. "Look at me, Elena."

She didn't want to; she was afraid what the impact of looking at him would do to her, but he'd commanded she gaze up, and she had no choice.

Slowly her head lifted; the shot to her stomach when she made eye contact was more intense with him so close — more intense after what had happened the night before.

"Hmm." The low murmur vibrated off his lips, but he said nothing more. She had no idea what he was thinking.

"Thank you for dinner," she finally said, though nothing was on her plate yet.

"You know this isn't about food." It was a statement.

"I don't know what this is about," she responded.

"Did you enjoy the show last night, Elena?"

Her mouth opened and she gazed at him, not knowing how to respond. She had felt he knew she'd been there, and now he was confirming it. Her cheeks flushed scarlet as she cast her gaze down. She was mortified and wanted more than anything to get up and run away.

"No, I didn't see you, but I knew exactly where you were," he said, his voice a low rumble. Her stomach stirred. How that was possible, she didn't know.

"I'm ... uh ... I'm sorry. I wasn't trying to spy on you. I was outside, and then you appeared, and it was too late to leave." She stumbled over her words as she tried to quickly get them out.

"I didn't mind you being there," he said, his eyes and voice almost predatory. "In fact, I was glad you were. I could *feel* you watching, enjoying as I climaxed."

She gasped at his words, not understanding the instant wetness she felt below. She squeezed her legs together and shifted in her seat, and his eyes brightened as if he knew exactly what was going on with her. She was once again locked on his gaze. No matter how much she wanted to turn away, she couldn't.

"Did you come, Elena? Did you pleasure yourself?" he asked, making her cheeks heat even more. He leaned forward the tiniest bit. "I think you did. I felt your desire through the air, your arousal. I felt the pleasure coursing through you, and it sent me to a whole new level of excitement. I could practically taste you on my lips."

She said nothing as his voice washed over her. It was amazing what was happening to her. The same feeling she'd felt the night before was rushing through her body, her core wet, her legs squeezing together to try to relieve the pressure. She was sure he could see the hardness of her nipples through the thin material of the dress but there was nothing she could do to stop it.

"Do you not have anything to say to that, Elena?" he asked, his lips slightly mocking.

"No, sir," she responded, wanting desperately to look down, but unable to break contact with his eyes.

"You're feeling it now, Elena. I can smell your arousal. I can see the dilation in your eyes. Your body is so responsive to just words and sights. I wonder what it will do when I actually touch you, taste you, plunge deep inside you."

The more he spoke, the harder her heart beat, the more flushed her skin became.

"Do you want me to do all of that to you, Elena?"

He finally leaned back, but she still felt as if she were trapped inside his tiny bubble. And that wasn't the worst place to be.

"No, sir," she finally said, knowing it was a lie. She wanted that more than she wanted oxygen.

"I think you're lying to me, but I'll let you get away with it for now," he said with a short laugh.

She stayed silent.

"Would you like some wine?"

"I've never had wine," she told him. She'd seen bottles in the wine cellar, but she'd never tasted it.

"Then this will be a real treat for you," he told her.

He rang a bell, and within seconds, someone entered the room with a chilled dark bottle. The server never glanced in Elena's direction, just poured a splash into Dalton's glass and waited for his boss to approve it.

After the server filled both glasses, he told Dalton he would serve the food shortly. Dalton said nothing as the man left then returned quickly with soup and bread.

The aroma drifting her way made her mouth water. She'd never eaten anything that smelled that good. Still, she gripped her hands in her lap. She wouldn't start until Dalton told her she could. That was a lesson she'd learned long ago — painfully.

"Eat, Elena," he said as he picked up his spoon.

The first bite was an explosion of flavors on her tongue, and Elena had to force herself to eat slowly. She would have picked the bowl up to drink it down, it was so delicious, but she knew that wouldn't go over well, so instead she filled the spoon half full and took small bites of her meal, setting the spoon down every couple of bites to pick up her glass of wine and take a sip.

Dalton was right. The wine was an incredible treat. She didn't notice when he continued filling the glass, keeping it full. Soon, she felt her body relaxing as Dalton's gaze held her eyes captive once again.

"Are you happy here, Elena?"

That was a loaded question if ever there was one. She squirmed in her seat and tried to figure out an acceptable response.

"I'm very well taken care of, sir. I have no complaints," she finally murmured.

He stared at her, his eyes narrowing the smallest bit. Her head was beginning to grow a bit fuzzy, making it harder and harder to think, making it tougher to maintain her composure.

He refilled her glass.

"Do you still get mistreated?"

"No, sir." She knew that's what she was supposed to say.

Without thinking about it, though, she ran her fingers across her cheek where it still stung from Leo's last hit.

Dalton's eyes narrowed as he closely examined her.

He picked up his phone. "Hold the rest of the meal until I call for it." He set down the phone and stood. She wasn't sure what to do now.

"Follow me, Elena."

Nerves rushed through her as she stood, and she found herself wobbling at the first step. Dalton quickly steadied her. The touch of his hand on her arm sent lightning through her skin, and she sucked in a breath. He paused for a minute as he looked down at her, his eyes narrowing again, and his lips parted as if he wanted to say something. Finally, he closed his mouth and led her into the next room.

Now, *this* was the bedroom. Her stomach clenched. Leo was going to kill her. But what could she do? She had no choice, no say in what happened in her life. If Dalton wanted to bed her, she couldn't say no. Even if she did, it would do her as much good as it did to fight Leo. Saying no only added more to her pain.

The difference was that she wasn't sick at the thought of Dalton taking her, doing to her what he'd talked about doing. The only thing holding her back was the beating Leo was sure to give her if it happened.

Dalton moved to where two large chairs were sitting by a fireplace. With the click of a button the fire roared to life and instant heat warmed her skin. He stood in front of the chairs.

"Turn around," he told her.

Shaking, Elena did as he said. She didn't want this. Didn't want another man to take her, especially a man she actually felt something for. Not while she still had fresh bruises from an hour before, not while she was still sore from the rough treatment she'd just received.

But Dalton's hands were on the zipper of her dress, and she felt it loosening. She tried to stop her body from trembling as the dress began falling off her shoulders, tried to stop the tears, but one escaped anyway.

When the dress dropped to the floor, Dalton turned her around and looked at her face, his finger lifting as he gently wiped the tear away. Then he knelt in front of her and grasped her waist, looking at her body.

His fingers traced over her skin, and she winced when he found the tender bruises. She could barely stand as he knelt before her. He was silent for so long she was confused as to what was happening. This was never something Leo had done with her.

"You will tell me now who has done this," he said, the fury in his voice making her knees shake.

"I don't understand," she stuttered. But she did. She knew exactly what he was asking.

His fingers slid across a particularly large bruise, and she winced again.

"If you try to lie to me, it won't go well," he threatened.

Elena shook before him, not knowing what to do. Her throat closed, and she could no longer stop the tears from falling as Dalton stood back up and gripped her shoulders. She was between a rock and a hard place. Elena wasn't sure who she feared more — Leo or Dalton.

Dalton had never hurt her, but she'd barely spent any time with the man. And there was something about him that was dark and threatening, but at the same time it drew her in, making her want to confide in him.

She knew for sure that Leo was willing to hurt her.

So she chose not to speak at all. For that matter, she couldn't speak as her emotions came to a head, and she finally broke down. It had to be the wine, or the lack of sleep, or any number of reasons. Whatever it was, the dam broke and she shattered.

Dalton looked up, surprise on his face as she completely let go, something she'd never done before. Normally she was able to hold it in until she was alone, and even then she'd never sobbed this hard.

Finally he got up and sat, pulled her onto his lap, and he held her silently as she sobbed without speaking a word, until darkness eventually gave her the relief the tears wouldn't.

CHAPTER THIRTY-THREE

BLINKING HER PUFFY eyes, Elena slowly woke and sat up as she looked around. She didn't know where she was.

The shadowy figure sitting next to the bed alerted her she wasn't alone. Her breathing came out in short pants as she tried to get her bearings. Her mind flashed through the night before, though it was all a little hazy.

Maybe she wasn't meant to be a wine drinker.

"Have you calmed down?"

The cold fury in Dalton's voice made her shiver. She wasn't sure who the rage was directed at, but as she was the only person in the room with him, she could take a good guess it was her.

"I'm sorry. I don't know why I fell apart," she told him.

"I want to know what has happened to you, Elena."

She was quiet for several heartbeats and could practically feel the rage flowing from Dalton, coming off him in waves and hitting her with their force. She wasn't trying to enrage the man, but she also wasn't so foolish as to give him the information he was demanding.

"This is simply a part of my life, sir. I don't see why you're asking me about it. I live in *your* home with *your* staff," she said, a touch of anger igniting in her voice.

It might have been the wrong tone to use with him, because suddenly the shadows were pushed aside as he jumped to his feet, switched on the lamp, and towered over her in the bed. His eyes were violent as he looked down at her.

Everything that possibly could have happened to her over the years had already occurred, so Elena simply looked back at him, deciding she wasn't going to cower this time. Maybe her misery would end if she were defiant enough.

That thought led to a flashback as memories began to flood her. She'd given up once before. Closing her eyes, she remembered angering one of the men who loved to punish her. She hadn't gotten the concussion the way Leo had told her she had.

Lies!

Everything Leo had spoken to her about had been nothing but lies. But as she remembered more and more, fear filled her again. She knew what the consequences were for disobeying, for pushing men around.

It didn't end her life, but it made her feel like she wanted her life ended. She trusted Dalton no more than she trusted anyone in her world. She needed time to think, but that wasn't possible.

"You dare speak to me this way in my own home?" Dalton finally asked through clenched teeth, making her very much aware of his presence once again.

"I don't know what you want me to say, so I spoke my mind," she told him. Where had this backbone come from?

Elena was used to living in fear so she wasn't quite sure.

"You will tell me what happened to you."

"I won't."

She crossed her arms stubbornly against her chest, and he leaned back, sheer surprise lighting his face.

"You won't leave this room until you decide to talk."

He stood up and began walking away. She didn't think he was bluffing. But then again, she didn't know what else to do.

"Sir . . ." she yelled out but then stopped. What was she going to say?

"Are you ready to speak?" he asked from the doorway.

"No. It's just that I have a job to do," she told him.

His eyes widened slightly at her statement. Then he blanked his expression as he finished walking to the door. He opened it then turned back to her.

"I will come back tomorrow. Maybe you will have come to your senses by then."

With that, he walked out and shut the door. She heard a lock turning.

The echo of a locking door flooded her with new memories of being carelessly tossed in her room, freezing and malnourished, while a door was tightly secured. What hell was this place? And where did she really belong? Elena didn't know. She knew nothing.

She looked around her new prison and wondered if he truly thought this was punishment. The bed was soft, far more luxurious than the one she normally slept in. The floor space was huge, providing ample pacing room, and there was a door leading to what she hoped was a bathroom.

If this was her punishment for not talking, he would be very surprised when she didn't utter another single sound.

Getting out of bed, she moved to the doorway and smiled when she saw the large soaking tub in the corner of the bathroom.

Yes, let the punishment begin.

She stripped after drawing her bathwater then sank below the bubbles she'd added. Worry was still with her, but it was nothing more than a slight whisper.

Leo would be furious. Elena wondered if he would come to her room. She wondered if Dalton would allow it. If Leo did come, though, he surely wouldn't hit her. He wouldn't dare. Not with the boss watching so closely.

She finished her bath, got out, went in the bedroom, and found a nightgown and robe on the bed. No other clothes than those.

Fine. She would wear the clean nightgown. It didn't appear as if she was doing anything other than lying around all day.

At noon a woman she'd never met before brought her lunch without saying a word, then left, locking the door behind her. Elena was very aware of the large man waiting in the doorway while the maid was there. It appeared as if Dalton wasn't taking any chances on her running.

It occurred to her that he might be protecting her. Why would he want to do that? She was nothing more than a female body to him.

There was nothing to do in the room: no books, no television . . . nothing. By nightfall, Elena was thinking this wasn't such a great punishment after all. She hadn't gotten to go outside, and though she moved to the window and looked out, it wasn't the same.

Leo didn't come to her. That was one thing she was grateful for. Dalton also didn't come back that day. She wasn't happy about that. Although, she should be.

Finally, after tossing and turning for several hours, Elena found peace in sleep. Maybe the next day would go better. She'd never know until it arrived.

CHAPTER THIRTY-FOUR

ELENA COULDN'T BREATHE. Her eyes snapped open as she fought against the hand pinning her nose together while trapping her mouth. Her hands came up, and she scratched at the person trying to end her life, but it was to no avail. Her feet kicked out, and she would have screamed if she could have drawn in air.

Fighting did no good. Slowly, her vision began to grow blurry as blackness started taking over. Stars flashed brightly but then began dimming. Her limbs fell to her sides as she lost strength to fight her attacker.

Fear morphed into relief. Death had to be better than the life she was living. Her limbs went numb, and a tiny smile flitted across her lips as she welcomed the abyss. No one would hit her anymore, or force themselves upon her. No one would demand answers she wasn't at liberty to give and maybe, just maybe, she would find the child that visited her in her dreams.

It was over. It was finally over.

When Elena woke up, she thought for one moment that she was in heaven. There wasn't any pain or fear. She was warm and comfortable. But before she opened her eyes, she stiffened.

Heaven was still out of reach. She wasn't even close to it. Maybe people like her didn't get there. That was probably the case. Elena knew she was still in hell, and she knew the lord and master of her personal hell was sitting there with her.

"See how easy it would be for me to take your life."

A shudder passed through Elena.

"I've always known my life was in your hands," she told Leo.

"Then why are you risking it?" he questioned.

He moved closer to her on the bed and ran a hand through her hair. She wanted to scream, wanted to push him away, but she knew better. They were alone. And Dalton moving her hadn't meant anything.

Obviously Leo had gotten through the locks, had snuck past whatever roadblocks had been put into place. There was nowhere she was safe — near or far. Her life was in Leo's hands, and he'd shown her how quickly he could take her to the brink of death, only to stop at the last moment, so he could do it over and over again.

"I'm not trying to," she told Leo. "I didn't say anything to Dalton. He was furious with me. That's why I've been locked in here."

"How did he know there was a problem?" Leo snapped.

Elena reached up and felt her cheek where a slight bruise remained.

"He saw the bruising," she told him, refusing to shake anymore. She willed her body not to react to this angry man.

"Did he fuck you? Is that how he saw them?" Leo snarled.

The hand that had been caressing her hair was now fisting it. It took all her strength not to whimper at the new pain he was causing.

"No. I swear he didn't have sex with me," she assured him.

His hand loosened. "That's good. But I can see that's what he plans," Leo snapped.

"I don't think so. I really don't," she said, but she wasn't sure of that. She'd say just about anything to keep Leo from losing his temper.

"You didn't think I wanted you either, Elena. You're not the brightest when it comes to men and their desires," he said with a quiet, sinister laugh. "I've seen the way he looks at you. Just because he has all the money in the world he thinks he's entitled to whatever he wants. You're mine! I don't like sharing what's mine."

He suddenly pulled her up and sat her on his naked lap, already hard. He always grew hard when he roughed her up.

"I got excited watching you struggle as I cut off your air," he said, the wicked light in his eyes unmistakable.

What was she supposed to say to that? *Thank you?* Never! She might appear to be broken to all these people, but somewhere deep inside she wanted her freedom. She still wanted to find out who she was. She would play their games, but she planned on being the ultimate victor — even if she had moments of defeat. When she wasn't being beaten to within an inch of her life, she struggled. Still, she remained quiet as he grasped the bottom of her nightgown and pulled it over her head, tossing it aside.

"Aren't you worried Dalton will come in?" she asked.

It was the wrong thing to say because fury contorted Leo's face as he gripped her hips and pulled her closer to him, his hardness embedded in her exposed core.

"Don't you dare say that man's name when you are naked in my arms," he snapped as he reached up and squeezed her breast hard enough that she let out a cry.

He leaned forward and bit her lip for making the sound. Not enough to break the skin and leave evidence he'd been there, but enough to make it hurt.

"I'm sorry." She knew she needed to apologize, or he would keep punishing her.

"You *are* sorry, aren't you, Elena? You're a sorry excuse for a woman. If you weren't so good-looking, didn't have a terrific body, you would have been thrown out long ago like the trash you are," he said, taking delight in putting her down.

How could he profess to love her one moment and then be so cruel the next? This was why Elena wanted nothing to do with love.

She wanted to lash out at him, scream, slap him. Tell him he was a worthless pig. But she did none of that. Was it basic survival skills? She wasn't sure. But whatever it was, she remained motionless in his arm.

"You like me being deep inside you, don't you, whore?" he asked while pounding upward in a painful way.

"Yes, Leo," she said, knowing there wasn't another answer he would accept.

"I know you do," he said with a chuckle as he continued invading her body. She was silent since that hadn't been a question.

He leaned forward and bit into her nipple, and this time she didn't utter a sound as pain washed through her. It was odd how when Dalton had touched her breasts she'd felt pleasure fill her, but all she ever felt from Leo was pain.

What was the difference?

Sure, Leo enjoyed hurting her, especially when he didn't get the response he felt he deserved, but any man's touch should disgust her. Somehow Dalton's didn't, though. Maybe she was just that messed up in the head, that she would enjoy the other man's attention.

When Leo flipped her onto her back and began to find a quick release at her expense, she withdrew to another place. The video of her and her father playing on the beach. The sand looked so warm, the water incredibly inviting.

That's where she always went. She closed her eyes and pretended to be on the beach while Leo grunted on top of her. She could almost feel the sun's warm rays heating her skin, could almost believe she was there instead of here, in her personal hell.

The nice thing with Leo, it never took him long to finish. She understood why he had to force her into a sexual relationship, because he would have a difficult time getting anyone to do what he wanted willingly.

Although he wasn't the worst looking man, or he hadn't been until he'd turned into the monster he was, his personality sucked. He had nothing to offer a partner.

Elena listened to the other staff members speak. She never joined in their conversations, but she listened to them gossip. All the staff thought Dalton was incredibly good-looking, a real catch. She'd heard whispers that most of the women were unsure if it was worth it to be with him, though, since he was kinky in the bedroom.

Elena didn't know what that meant. But unlike the rest of the staff, she knew she was different. She knew she didn't have the same freedom they did. She didn't know why, but they were allowed to come and go. They liked one another.

She, on the other hand, was trapped. She couldn't think for herself, couldn't voice an opinion, and couldn't be part of the club. It was a sad life, one she had given up trying to understand.

Leo finished with a low groan and then rolled off her only to turn on his side and slide his fingers against her smarting skin. He slipped a finger inside her bruised core and roughly pumped for a few moments just in case she hadn't already had enough. Then he slid his wet fingers up her body and pinched her nipple. Elena remained quiet, knowing he would grow bored with this soon enough and then she would be allowed to clean his disgusting scent off her.

"I have to go now. Dalton was called away on an emergency, but he'll be back soon. It was the reason I was able to get in here. But I needed to remind you that I *can* get to you. Even if it takes a long time, I will always get to you. Even if you tell Dalton I'm the one who gave you the bruises, I will find a way to get to you — telling him will be the last thing you ever do."

Leo rolled over her again so fast there was no chance to protect herself as he pinned her to the bed beneath him, his spit hitting her face while he snarled his words.

"I won't tell him, Leo."

That wasn't something she could promise though, because she didn't know if it was possible. Dalton was a determined man. What was really the worst thing that could happen if she told Dalton?

The worst thing wasn't death. She would welcome death. No. The worst thing was if Leo hot ahold of her and dragged her away to some place he could inflict all the torture he wanted, day and night.

It really wasn't worth the risk of telling Dalton. If she thought it would give her freedom she would. She owed nothing to Leo.

But she didn't think it would earn her anything more than extra trouble.

And going from one fire to another didn't help her. She would most likely get burned that much more.

CHAPTER THIRTY-FIVE

THE LOCK ON the bathroom door gave Elena a false sense of security. There was also a lock on her bedroom door, and yet Leo had still managed to get through with no problem at all, and get to her, wrap his hands around her throat, and nearly end her life.

Ending her life would never be enough for Leo, though. No. He enjoyed humiliating her, hurting her, and taking her against her will. How had she ever thought that man could be her savior? He'd been so different when she'd first come to know him — gentle, giving, and protective.

That had changed quickly after the master had died.

So even if she did feel something for Dalton, did it really matter? Wouldn't he turn out just like Leo? One minute he might be acting as if he was there to protect her, but then the next, he would turn on her. They all would.

It had been two days since Leo had paid her a visit, and she was still frightened of being in the new room. It was late when Elena let the bathwater drain from the tub then took her time toweling herself off.

She didn't bother bringing her nightgown into the bathroom. She was alone all the time. Dalton made his regular stops to the room, but always early. She assumed he was away from the house until late each night.

That was for the best. Nighttime was when she felt the weakest — the most vulnerable. It was when she desperately wanted to cling to someone to help her — save her. Though she wasn't even sure what she wanted saved from.

Definitely she didn't want to be with Leo anymore, and anyone who could save her from him would be a god in her book. But beyond that she just wanted to know who she was.

Wrapping the warmed towel around her body, she opened the bathroom door and stepped out. She was five steps into the room when she figured out she wasn't alone.

Every survival instinct inside her told her to run back into the bathroom and lock the door. But Elena knew she wouldn't make it. Then she would be in even worse trouble for running.

The room was dark, only lit by the half-moon shining in through the windows, but she could see the man sitting near her bed in the corner of her room. She almost let out a sigh of relief when she realized it was Dalton and not Leo.

But then she came to her senses and realized he was just as dangerous as Leo — maybe even more so, since she didn't know exactly what Dalton was capable of yet.

Elena didn't move forward as she looked in his direction, wishing she could see his expression to at least be prepared for what sort of mood he was in. She then glanced at the bed where her nightgown was laid out. Why hadn't she just taken it in the bathroom with her? She should always assume that someone could enter the room and lie there in wait for her.

She felt too vulnerable in nothing but the thick white towel that actually covered her pretty decently. Shifting from one foot to the other, she waited to find out what Dalton wanted.

"Come here, Elena," he finally said. Nothing in his tone gave away why he was in her room so late.

"I need to get dressed," she said, her voice hoarse as she moved toward her nightgown instead of doing what he demanded.

"No you don't," he told her. "I said to come here."

There was such command in his voice that her feet literally stopped moving toward the bed, instead stepping around it and going over to where he sat. She hated that she was so trained to do what she was told.

"That's better," he said in approval. And dammit, the praise made her glow a little bit. She didn't want to be pleased that she'd made him happy.

"Closer, Elena," he said quietly.

Shivering, she shuffled forward until she could practically feel the heat waves coming off his covered skin.

"Take off the towel."

It took a moment for the words to process, but once they did, she shivered again, this time in fear — and unbelievably, a bit of excitement.

"I don't want to," she said, her words almost too quiet to hear.

"Don't make me say it again," he said, his voice still low, but this time there was no mistaking the command.

Elena glared down at him, not sure if he could see the expression in the darkened corner of her room. But then she reached up and pulled at where the towel was tucked in against her chest. Letting go, it dropped to her feet, leaving her standing naked before him.

It was dark, but enough light was there that he could see her outline at least. She couldn't prevent the goosebumps crisscrossing over her skin.

He reached out, and she felt his hand on her hip as he tugged her forward so she was now standing between his spread thighs. She was only inches from his body. He lifted the other hand and it rested at her throat.

Her breathing quickened as he began moving downward with a soft caress. When his fingers skimmed over first one breast and then the other, she had to suck in the sound trying to escape. Her nipples beaded and ached at the light touch. She didn't want to show him that she was enjoying his touch though. It was a violation no matter how good it felt.

He continued moving his fingers down her body, swiping them along her stomach and then tracing the front of her thighs.

She felt wetness heat her core as he neared that area, but he didn't touch her *there*.

His fingers on her hip tightened and Elena found herself leaning forward before she stopped herself. But Dalton tugged her and then she was pressed against him, his face positioned between her breasts.

"I can't stop thinking about you, Elena, how you felt in my arms, how you smelled, the taste of your mouth . . ."

She was a wreck as he whispered the words against her skin.

His hot breath sent another shudder through her before he gripped her backside and tugged a little more. She felt his lips skim the underside of her breasts before he moved up and then his hot tongue swept across one nipple and then the other.

She waited for the pain of his bite, but it never came. He just moved from one breast to the other, his tongue laving over them before his lips tightened on them and he sucked, making her core pulse.

She felt moisture on her thighs as she trembled in his arms.

When he pulled back from her she wanted to protest, but amazingly managed to stop herself. His breathing was hot and heavy against her stomach as she stood between his thighs and waited for what came next.

"Are you ready to talk to me yet?" he asked, his voice almost gentle as he rubbed the cheeks of her butt.

She almost opened up and told him everything in her aroused state, only managing to stop herself at the last possible second. He sighed against her skin.

"I can give you so much pleasure if you do what I ask," he said, this time sounding irritated.

That snapped her from her dazed stupor, and she tugged against him, trying to get away. His fingers clenched on her butt cheeks, showing her she was only free to go when he allowed it.

"I don't want anything you have to give me," she said. If only her voice was more firm.

His fingers clenched against her skin again for a moment, and then she was surprised when he let her go. Quickly she stepped back, trying to cover herself, though it was still dark in this corner.

When he stood, she stepped back even farther.

"I'm not a patient man, Elena," he warned as he began moving, making her feel like a caged animal. "And I'll warn you that I'm just about at the end of my lenience."

She didn't say anything, not knowing what she could possibly do to explain why she wasn't telling him anything. Luckily she didn't have to. He turned and strode from the room.

Elena dressed quickly and then lay on her bed shivering, not understanding at all what had just happened. She didn't sleep that night.

CHAPTER THIRTY-SIX

THE NEXT DAY Elena was tense as she kept gazing at the door, wondering if, or when, Dalton was going to come back to see her. As the day turned to night, she then felt tense, unsure if either Dalton or Leo would come to her. The stress was almost more than she could bear.

When the clock kept on ticking, unbearably slow, she felt as if she couldn't move. She was too nervous to go into the bathroom again, not knowing what would be on the other side of the door when she came out. She wasn't afraid of Dalton — she was afraid of what he expected of her — of what she wanted to be when he was around.

Leo, on the other hand, she was terrified of. He had turned on a dime, and no longer was he the anchor in storm that grounded her. He was now her worst nightmare. When midnight hit, Elena decided that maybe she was free for the night. She wasn't sure if she felt a smidgeon of disappointment that Dalton hadn't come back to her or not.

He had awoken something in her and she felt shame that she wanted to explore it. There was so much wrong with that, which meant there was something *seriously* wrong with her. Maybe she'd been broken for a long time, and maybe it was Leo who had destroyed her. She wasn't sure.

When the lock on the door made a sound, she sat up in bed, clutching her blankets tightly against her as she waited to see who would enter. Only her bedside lamp was on low, and she waited as the door began to open. She forgot to even breathe.

When it was Dalton who stepped through the opening, Elena realized the relief that flooded through her. Not just because she wasn't going to have to endure more of Leo's torture for the night, but also because she had missed Dalton. She didn't know how that was possible.

Dalton moved over to her bed, his eyes intense as he sat down, immediately reaching for the blankets she was clutching so desperately. He tugged on them and she didn't release them. His eyes narrowed and she let go.

"Are you ready to talk yet?" he asked. How did he manage to maintain such control in his voice? She didn't understand it, but she instantly wanted to obey his every command. It was so different from how she felt with other people. The will to fight left her. There was something so secure about being with him.

"I can't," she whispered, hating that she was disappointing him.

His expression didn't change. He continued to study her, and she wondered if the man could read her thoughts. It was alarming, and she wanted to hide, but there was nowhere for her to go.

"That's disappointing," he said. His fingers rubbed along her collarbone and she felt shivers spreading throughout her frame. With the slightest of touches from this man, she came undone. She wanted to resent him for the act, but she couldn't.

"Is it that you like being hurt?" he asked.

Elena was shocked by his words. Was it true? Did she feel that she needed to be punished? Every time Leo violated her, was there a part of her that accepted it as what she deserved?

"No, I don't think I do," she said, trying to be as honest as she knew how to be.

His expression changed and he looked at her with what appeared to be wonder. He began undoing her nightgown, one tiny button at a time. She didn't try to stop him. His fingers whispered over her skin as she waited to see what he would do next.

"Do you know the difference between pleasure and pain?" he asked.

Elena wasn't sure where this conversation was going. It was all so odd. These weren't the type of questions she was normally asked.

"I don't know what you want me to say," she told him.

He continued undoing her nightgown until he reached the last button, the material sliding apart, revealing her breasts and the panties that didn't cover much. She wasn't sure if she wanted him to go on or if she wanted him to stop.

His large hand splayed across her chest before he ran it down her stomach, stopping at the lacy edge of her panties before going back up again. She shivered as desire shot through her.

"It's pretty clear, Elena. Do you know what *pain* is? What *pleasure* is?" he said, enunciating each word.

"Yes, I guess so," she said slowly. "One hurts, the other doesn't."

Dalton smiled at her, and she felt joy that she might have pleased him. But he shook his head, and her joy instantly diminished. She didn't know what she'd said wrong.

"Pleasure and pain can go hand in hand. But pleasure is intense, satisfying and needed," he told her.

"I don't see how they go hand in hand," she told him. There had been no pain that had been inflicted on her that she could say was also pleasurable. A challenge seemed to light in Dalton's eyes as his smile grew.

He leaned down and ran his tongue across her nipple, then pulled the peak into his mouth and bit down. A shiver of pain ran through her, but before it grew uncomfortable, he sucked the puckered skin and a shot of pleasure ran straight to her core. He leaned back.

"Pain and pleasure can be administered in such a way that you will never want to come down. You played with yourself that night I was in the gazebo. You watched me, saw my desire, felt the yearning in the air, and you made yourself come," he knowingly said.

"I didn't ..." She stopped as she tried to catch her breath as he flicked her nipple. "I didn't know what I was doing. It just ... it just happened." Elena wasn't sure why she was speaking so openly to him. He inspired her to do it, she supposed.

"Then maybe you need a lesson. Maybe if you understand that you don't have to be abused, that there are many other ways, maybe then you will talk to me," he told her.

He pulled his hand away and she bit her lip to keep from whimpering. She'd never imagined wanting a man on top of her — not after what Leo had done to her — but now it was hard to imagine not wanting it.

"It's very simple, Elena. If something is painful — truly painful — then you stop, you don't do it. You want to feel maximum pleasure. I want you to touch yourself. I want you to understand your body. There's no way for you to know what's good and what isn't if you don't know what you like."

"I don't want to touch myself," she said, her cheeks flushing in embarrassment. When she'd been hidden in the bushes, out of sight, thinking he didn't know she was there, it had been different. There was no way she could do what he was expecting while his eyes watched every movement she made.

Dalton stood up, pulled his shirt over his head, then undid his pants. Elena's mouth watered as he pulled them down, his body hard everywhere, but her eyes were drawn to the part of him that was thick and solid, long and beautiful. She ripped her gaze back to his face, but he smiled cockily at her. He knew she was impressed. She hated him for knowing it.

He sat back down on the bed, this time leaning against her headboard, his leg brushing hers as he placed his fingers around his thickness and moved them up and down his long shaft. She couldn't tear her eyes away. A bead of moisture appeared at the tip and he rubbed it down his length before moving back up again.

"You have to know how to touch yourself or you can't show someone how to do it," he told her. Elena's core was throbbing as blood rushed through her. She wanted to be like that woman at the gazebo, wanted to lean down and take a taste of him. She wouldn't dare do something so bold though.

"It's important for you to relax, to fantasize while you lie alone in bed, and to be comfortable with yourself. There's nothing wrong with it," Dalton continued. "You can take a long bath, then rub lotion all across your skin. You can then dress in something sexy, feeling the caress of satin and lace rubbing against you. Maybe you put on nothing at all but a tasty scent. All of it is sexy, all of it will get you in the mood."

"Dalton, this isn't going to happen," she told him, surprised at how husky her voice was.

He smiled at her again. "It's going to happen," he said. "You can do this with me, or I can march you naked through the house and see who appears to either claim you as his, or who gives you a look of murder. I can take you to the living room and fuck you right there and see who comes along. We do things my way, or you will answer me now — one way or the other."

He was calm as he spoke, didn't hesitate with a single word. She knew it wasn't a bluff. Dalton wasn't afraid of what anyone would think if he did exactly as he said he would. She looked away in defeat. He'd won, and they both knew it.

"Lie down," he told her. She felt an odd sense of desire as she did what he requested. She scooted down in the bed and laid flat on her back, her gown parted, her body exposed.

"If you were all alone doing this, then you would fantasize about a lover, someone who turns you on. You would pretend he's the one touching you, spreading you wide open and licking and sucking his way across your body." She shivered at his words. It felt almost as if he was doing everything he was saying.

"Just relax, Elena. Spread your legs open," he told her. "You need to feel vulnerable. You need to remember you can have anything you want."

She stopped fighting him. She was powerless to do so. She turned her head, his thick erection in his hand, dripping his pleasure out as he gazed at her body and stroked himself.

"I don't feel like I can have anything I want," she told him. Still, she followed his instructions.

"Maybe you just need the right person to lead you there," he said. "Reach up and cup your breasts, picturing me doing it. See what feels right. Squeeze your nipples and feel them harden, feel what that does to the rest of your body." She did as he said and her body trembled as her eyes closed and she moaned at the sensation rushing through her.

"Do you like it when I touch you, Elena?" he asked. He'd laid down, his face beside hers, his hot breath rushing over her. She trembled as she ached to reach out for him. "Are your nipples hard and aching, sensitive to the touch?"

"Yes," she said on a sigh, completely lost in this moment with him. How she ached for him to replace her own hands.

"Very good. This is all good," he said, his voice husky. He sped up the speed of stroking himself, the sound of his hand squeezing his thick member echoed in the room, making her thighs shake.

"You are so damn sexy. It's almost impossible for me not to touch you," he told her.

"Why don't you?" she asked before she bit her lip to keep her from begging him to do exactly that.

"I am showing you what pleasure I can give you if you let go," he said. The feel of his hot breath was driving her insane. "Now reach down, slowly slip off your panties."

That last scrap of material was her final guard and she didn't want to take it away. But even feeling that way, she reached down, hooked her thumbs inside the lace and slowly pulled them off her legs. Then she waited.

He was silent for several moments as he moved on the bed. She felt his breath as he moved above her, not touching her. His breath hit her between the legs and she arched off the bed as she reached for him. She wanted his mouth on her. He moved away instead.

"Open your legs wide. You are so responsive, so wet and slick," he told her, his voice deep and rough. A groan escaped him and she felt the pressure build inside her. "Reach down, Elena, rub your fingers over your wet folds, slip them inside and feel the way your body is responding to my words, to your touch."

Her body reacted as she slid her fingers around her folds, slipped them inside. She was so hot, so wet, so needy. Her fingers moved to where it felt the best and she circled the throbbing piece of flesh as she moaned, her back arching.

"Are you getting close, Elena? Do you feel the pressure building?" he asked. She heard the sound of him again stroking himself as he panted. He was kneeling between her thighs. She opened her eyes and looked at him.

He was magnificent. His chest gleamed with a sheen of sweat, his eyes were dilated as he gazed at her spread thighs, watched as she stroked herself. His hand moved faster as he rubbed his entire length, moisture slipping from his pulsing head.

"You are so beautiful, so damn sexy," Dalton told her. He stoked himself faster and she sped up the circles she was making on her sensitive flesh. "I want you to make yourself come, Elena. Rub fast and hard, feel the pressure build, feel it get ready to explode. Don't try to stop it," he demanded.

Her movements were in tune with his. She stoked faster as she watched his hand move up and down his length. His eyes never left her. They roamed from her wet and sensitive core, to her breasts, her lips, her eyes. She'd never felt anything close to this with Leo. She only wanted Dalton.

"Come with me now, Elena," he commanded.

Elena flicked her flesh and felt the explosion rip through her. Her entire body tensed as she shook, the waves of pleasure coming over her repeatedly as she continued stroking her flesh. Dalton let out a cry as his fist slid over his hardness.

Then she watched him through her narrowed eyes as his pleasure shot from him, the warm fluid touching her stomach. They shook together as their orgasms raced through them. When it was over, Elena felt vulnerable and exposed.

She reached for her blankets, trying to cover herself, but Dalton stopped her as he leaned over her, his face close to hers. He wouldn't allow her to look away. Elena couldn't even explain what had just happened.

"Don't keep fighting me, or hiding from me. Talk to me, tell me what I need to know. There is a lot we can do together," he told her.

Elena didn't say a word. He looked disappointed, but he didn't say anything else. He moved off her bed and gathered up his clothes. Elena grabbed the blankets and shook beneath them as she stared at him.

"There are a lot of monsters in this world. Some would say I'm one of them. I can either be your friend, or your enemy. I guarantee you, you won't want me as the later."

"I can't tell you," she said, a few tears slipping from her eyes.

"You will," he promised.

He gave her one more intense stare, then he slipped from her room. Elena ran her hands over her body again. She couldn't believe what she'd just done. It had been incredible, but now that the moment was over, she was embarrassed. Sex seemed to take something from a person, left them too vulnerable.

She didn't like that. She also didn't know what she was going to do next. She just hoped for sleep to take her away. It was the only time she found any peace.

CHAPTER THIRTY-SEVEN

COULD A PERSON die of boredom? Elena wondered if there were any cases. Never would she have imagined she'd wish for the days of scrubbing floors and surfaces, or being slapped around, but she would almost prefer that to being locked in a bedroom day and night. She wondered if she might be going insane. Who truly needed sanity anyway? Maybe the world was a better place if you weren't fully aware of what was out there, what was going on.

She heard the doorknob turning to open her bedroom door, and she glanced at it with disinterest. One week she'd been in this room, and for that week, Dalton had come in at the same time every day, asking the same question.

Her reply never varied.

He hadn't made another midnight visit, and Elena wasn't sure if she was happy or sad about that. She tried telling herself she was glad, but nights were so lonely . . .

"Haven't you had enough, Elena?"

That wasn't what he normally asked. She turned to look at him. She was on a food strike, hadn't eaten in three days, her lunch sitting on her small table, untouched.

His eyes narrowed when he saw her condition. What did it matter? What did anything matter anymore? She'd come to a conclusion, since she had little time to do anything except think; there was no reason for her to go on.

She'd contemplated suicide. There were ways she could accomplish it. There were ties holding the curtains back. There was a chair. But something inside her rebelled at the thought of actually taking her own life. If she simply starved to death that wasn't suicide. It was just giving up. There was a difference.

"My maid informed me you haven't touched your food again today. That's going to stop now," Dalton said when she refused to answer his first question.

She still said nothing. What was the point in talking to him? She couldn't say what he wanted to hear, and he'd only grow angrier with her. At least she knew he wouldn't hit her, or he hadn't so far. Things could change. She'd once thought Leo was a good guy. She'd been proven wrong about that time and time again.

That was the one blessing in her imprisonment. Leo hadn't come back to her since that first night. Maybe security was tighter, or maybe he was busy, but whatever the reason, he hadn't returned. Her body was almost back to normal — whatever normal was.

She wouldn't know.

"When I speak to you, don't ignore me," Dalton thundered.

She turned and looked at him, her eyes blank. She had no energy, a blessing from not eating. She was sleeping a lot more. She didn't have to face as much time in each new day.

"I'm going to take a nap now," she said, her voice hoarse from lack of talking.

"No, you aren't. You're coming with me."

That surprised her.

"Going where?" She was almost interested. "Outside?" She hated the hope that had sprouted within her.

"Get up, and you will find out," he told her.

She didn't have the energy to move. Dalton walked over to the phone and spoke a few terse words into the receiver before hanging it up. Within a few minutes, the maid, who'd been serving her, came with a fresh tray of food.

She set it down and removed the other one before quietly slipping back out of the room. The aroma of warm soup and fresh bread drifted over to her. It was strange though. The longer she'd gone without eating, the less she cared about it. Normally the smell of a delicious meal would have had her mouth watering, as she was usually served little more than bread and crackers.

"If you want to go with me, you will eat," Dalton told her, moving to her chair and lifting her. She hung limply in his arms while he carried her to the table.

Should she break her fast and accept this new challenge? Surely she didn't have long to go before her body gave out if she just held steady.

"Elena, you *are* coming with me. If I phrased it like a question, I apologize for the misunderstanding," he said, though she knew this man apologized for nothing. He was simply using words he didn't mean. "You either eat this on your own, or I swear I will tie you to the chair and force-feed you."

His words were spoken almost conversationally. She was almost ready to challenge him. But she was too weak to find anything pleasant in that. Taking more energy than she realized, she picked up the spoon, dipped it in the bowl, leaned over, and took a sip of the hot chicken soup.

After the first bite, her taste buds came to life with a vengeance, her eyes widening and her stomach rumbling. Dalton no longer had to force her to eat. She cleaned the tray of food and still wanted more, but her shrunken stomach couldn't have handled more without heaving.

"Feeling better now?" he asked knowingly.

Yes, she was much better. Energy was returning, and she was able to sit up straighter. It still didn't mean she was ready to go anywhere with this man.

"I don't care how I feel, and I know you don't either," she told him, her voice coming back along with her temper.

"There you are," he said with the hint of a smile. "I like this Elena much better."

"I don't care what you like," she said with a glare.

He laughed at her, making her even more furious.

"I'll have clothes brought in. Shower and be ready in one hour."

He turned and left the room.

She thought about refusing. Bathing had been another thing she'd given up. She had hoped if she were disgusting enough, if Leo showed up, he'd be so repulsed he wouldn't want to touch her.

The reality was she could barely tolerate herself. And it had only been a few days. With a sigh, she rose and moved into the bathroom. She knew when she was finished the clothes would be on the bed. The staff seemed to know the minute the bathroom water came on. They would slip silently in and out of her room.

She didn't want to be excited, but Elena found she was as she took her time showering and getting dressed. Only thirty minutes had passed, and she was going slowly.

She sat back down in the chair by the window and tried not to continuously glance at the clock. She couldn't help but wonder where they were going — and how long they would be gone.

When the doorknob started turning again, her breath hitched in anticipation.

CHAPTER THIRTY-EIGHT

STILL NOT UP to full energy, Elena took her time moving from the bedroom. Maybe the food strike hadn't been such a great idea. She was less capable of fighting back now.

She felt odd traveling down the large staircase at Dalton's side. A couple of the servants looked up, surprise in their eyes, before they quickly averted their gaze. It didn't appear as if this was a common occurrence.

The boss probably didn't often walk with people beneath him on the social food chain. She decided it was much easier to look at the ground as they made their way forward.

"The car is ready, Sir."

She'd never seen this man before. His deep voice surprised her enough to look up. He was looking directly at Dalton, which gave her a moment to study him. He was older than her, maybe late thirties, and had the kindest eyes she'd ever encountered.

Elena found herself wanting to walk up to him, talk to him, have him tell her everything was going to be okay. She had no idea where those thoughts were coming from. It was strange.

"Thank you, Lincoln."

The man held open the front door, and Dalton held out his hand for her to step through before him. The bright glare of the sun made her squint, but a beaming smile overtook her face when she felt the warm rays on her skin.

It wasn't the same as sitting behind a window. There was nothing like fresh air, nothing like feeling the sun on her body, the little bit of wind biting into her cheeks, and hearing the sounds of birds tweeting up high.

She stopped too long, so Dalton ushered her forward, and she was reluctant to crawl into the backseat of the awaiting car. She just wanted a few more minutes.

Just as she was about to climb in, a chill ran through her, and she looked over to the edge of the house. Her eyes locked on Leo's. He was standing there with another man, and if looks could kill, she would be dead right on the spot.

A shiver traveled through her. Dalton didn't see the interaction take place, and she quickly looked down. She hoped Dalton was taking her far away, never to return. She hoped he was setting her free.

Of course, she didn't know where she would go. She had nothing: no money, no memories, no idea of what life was like outside of this property. She'd never stepped foot off it.

They got into the car and slowly made their way down a long tree-lined driveway until they approached a set of huge iron gates that began to part as they approached.

Elena had to fight not to look behind her. She wondered what Leo was going to do when she did return. She had no doubt they would be back. Dalton wasn't going to set her free. She hadn't earned that right.

If only Elena knew what she could do to gain freedom.

When they were past the gates, Elena let out a relieved breath. She glanced back, making sure Leo wasn't chasing them down. Of course, she knew he wouldn't — not when she was with Dalton. What she feared was when she wasn't with him. What would happen to her then?

They drove down a busy highway, and Elena had no idea where she was. She tried to look for clues. When they entered a freeway, she finally saw a sign. Seattle City Center, next exit.

She'd been taken all the way to the West Coast.

As soon as she had that thought, her mind began to spin. How did she know she was taken? How did she know she'd been transported a long way? Trembles began wracking her body as the car passed the exit and continued to move.

"Where are we going?" she asked, her voice small.

"Somewhere to talk," he replied.

"Are you going to kill me?"

There was utter silence to this question. She wasn't afraid. She would just rather know. If she knew a hit was coming, it wouldn't be such a shock to her system. If she knew she was going to die, she could say her final goodbyes to the voice that kept trying to pop into her head. She didn't know who the voice belonged to. She just knew she was someone else; this life hadn't been the one Elena had chosen.

"Why would you think I'm going to kill you?" he asked, pressing his fingers against her cheek and forcing her to look at him.

"The better question would be, why do you want to be near me?" she responded.

His eyes narrowed as he looked at her as if he was truly considering his answer.

"I don't know. There's something about you," he finally said. Then he released his grip on her, and she went back to staring out the window.

It appeared as if both their questions weren't going to be answered.

The car finally stopped after driving for well over an hour, and then the back door opened. Dalton stepped from the car and held out his hand for her. She didn't hesitate to take it and get out of the car.

When the ocean wind hit her face, Elena couldn't help the smile that appeared. Closing her eyes for a moment she enjoyed the mixture of heat and wind on her cheeks. Then she opened her eyes and took in the sunset right on the beach as the wind whipped her hair. It was a feeling unlike anything she'd ever experienced before.

Without waiting for permission, she began to move, reaching the edge of the sand. Barely taking time to remove her shoes, she dropped them on the edge of the sand, and then she ran.

Laughter escaped her throat, the sound foreign to her ears as she moved swiftly forward, not stopping until her feet splashed in the ocean. The icy-cold water was a shock, but her laughter didn't stop nor did she quit moving.

She turned so she was running along the edge of the water, the cold beads splashing up on her pants, making her feel more alive than she'd ever felt.

Elena had no idea how far she'd run when she couldn't catch her breath anymore, but finally she slowed, bending at the waist. She suddenly turned. No one had tried to stop her.

But there was Dalton, a couple feet away, an odd expression in his eyes as he watched her, like she was a puzzle he couldn't quite put together.

"I wasn't running from you," she told him. Now that her carefree sprint was over, she didn't want to feel any retaliation that would ruin this moment.

"I know," he said, his voice low, puzzled. "Your face has changed. There's a . . . a glow about you that is taking my breath away," he finished.

"I feel . . . free," she murmured. "Thank you for this."

Dalton stepped forward into the ankle deep water until he was right in front of her. His arms wrapped around her, and his head was only inches from hers.

"You are stunning," he gasped.

"I'm nothing special, Dalton," she told him. She didn't want another man obsessed with her. The last one still wouldn't let her go, and his obsession caused her all sorts of pain.

"That's where you're wrong, Elena. You're the type of woman wars begin over. You're the type of woman a man gets lost in," he whispered.

"Why? What do you see? I don't even know who I am," she said in almost a whimper.

"I do." The statement was quiet.

"What do you mean?"

He was silent as he gazed into her eyes, and she wanted to know what he was thinking, what was going on behind those dark black lashes.

"I know exactly who you are and where you came from. After my father died, I made sure to find out," he told her.

Elena nearly stumbled, but his arms were there to catch her. She searched his face to see if he was lying to her, but she couldn't see any hints of deceit.

"Who am I?" she finally asked.

"I don't think you really want the answer to that," he told her.

"Yes, I do!" she yelled as she lifted her fists and pounded on his chest.

"You tell me who's been hurting you, and I will tell you whatever you want to know," he said.

An ultimatum. She knew what that was. Her eyes narrowed, and she tried to tug away from him. This was all a lie. He had nothing to tell her. He just wanted answers, and he was willing to say or do anything to get what he wanted.

Suddenly his fist was bunched into the back of her hair as he pulled her body against his so she could no longer punch him or pull away. She glared into his eyes, and he smiled.

"I don't lose, Elena," he said as he leaned forward and nipped her bottom lip.

"You better start preparing yourself for a loss now so you're not devastated by it," she snapped.

Instead of anger, he threw back his head and laughed. She wanted to claw out his eyes and most likely would have if her arms weren't trapped between their bodies.

"I think it's time for me to show you exactly who *I* am," he said, fire igniting in his eyes.

"I know who you are," she told him.

"You have no clue, Elena, no clue at all," he warned.

"Do you think I'm afraid of you, Dalton? I've lived in fear a long time, and I refuse to ever be afraid again," she said.

"I don't want you to be afraid," he told her. "But I do want your respect," he said, his tone hard and commanding.

"You won't ever have it," she warned.

"We will see who comes out the winner."

Suddenly she was lifted into the air and flopped over his shoulder as he made his way back down the beach she'd enjoyed running along. She pounded her fists against his back, but after several minutes she was exhausted.

He didn't even breathe heavy as he confidently strode down the shoreline. It took them at least twenty minutes to reach the car, and when he set her back on her feet, she wobbled, her legs slightly numb from being carried caveman style.

When her eyes met Lincoln's in embarrassment, the man didn't show the slightest emotion as he held open the back door of the limousine.

"I'm not going anywhere with you," she told Dalton as she took a step back.

That statement only made him smile.

"Where do you think you'll go if not with me?" he asked, not seeming concerned.

"I don't care. Maybe I'll stay here on the beach," she stubbornly said.

He just smiled again before easily lifting her and practically tossing her in the car.

"I want full privacy, Lincoln," he said before following her in.

And then the door shut. Elena was once again the prey.

CHAPTER THIRTY-NINE

THE CAR BEGAN moving and Elena sat pressed to the door as if that would help her. If Dalton wanted something from her, he could take it. There would be no way for her to stop him.

She wasn't afraid of the man. She was far more fearful of herself and the reaction she had to him. It was nothing like what she felt for Leo. Once, Leo had been her protector and that had quickly shifted. Now she feared and loathed the guy.

Wouldn't it be the same with Dalton? Maybe at first she'd feel safe with him, but then he would suddenly become the enemy. She was learning that all men eventually did.

Elena didn't need to turn to know he was now sitting right next to her, not quite touching, but he was within inches of her body. A tremble began in her knees and slowly trailed out through the rest of her body as she remembered how easily he could make her melt.

Without saying a word, he leaned a little closer, his hot breath warming the side of her neck, making the small trembles increase like an 8.0 earthquake.

"Stop," she told him, wishing her voice was coming out a heck of a lot firmer instead of so damn husky.

"Why?" he responded, his warm breath caressing her ear and making her tighten her legs together to keep the ache from consuming her.

"I shouldn't need a reason," she told him. Though, that wasn't really true. She wasn't allowed a voice.

"Do you want me to stop because you're repulsed by me?" he asked. Before she could say a word, he continued. "Or do you want me to stop because you desire me, and it scares you?"

Her breathing was labored as she tried to form the lie on her lips that might actually make the man give her some breathing room.

When she said nothing, he moved her hair aside as his lips glided down the side of her neck while his hand climbed up the front of her shirt. Never had she felt this tightening when Leo had pawed all over her.

"Tell me to stop because you can't stand my touch," he growled as his hand moved up and cupped her breast, his strong fingers squeezing the tender nipple through her bra.

She panted beneath his touch trying to will her mouth to say the words that might make him stop this. But the only sound that came out was a small whimper when he quickly unfastened her bra and his fingers found her bare flesh.

She closed her eyes as she tried to will her body not to respond, but when his hand moved back down her stomach and undid her pants, she had to bite her lip to keep the moan from escaping.

He let go of her long enough to pull her pants down, although she attempted for a single moment to squeeze her legs together. He simply slid his hands down the front of her jeans and found her most tender area, making her legs turn to jelly.

Within a flash he pulled off all her clothes, and she found herself lying on her back along the limo's leather seat. The contrast of the cool leather against her hot skin only made her senses more heightened.

"I want to plunge inside you more than I want breath right now," he growled as he lay over her body, still fully clothed.

She wanted that too, but she couldn't — wouldn't — admit it to him.

He smiled down at her — a knowing, confident smile — before his lips crashed down on hers like a wave hitting rocks.

Without her being aware, her hands wound behind his head and gripped him, her hips thrusting upward, sounds escaping her throat that she didn't recognize as her own.

When he broke from her mouth she whimpered, but then his firm, hot lips were traveling down her throat, sucking and nipping hard at the skin, making her squirm beneath him.

When he took one of her ripe nipples into his mouth and sucked hard before gently biting down, she screamed in delight as she felt pressure continue building. He groaned against her skin before his lips continued their downward motion.

She writhed on the seat, nearly falling to the floor in her uninhibited ecstasy. He roughly spread her thighs wide open and before she could comprehend what he was doing, his mouth latched onto the place she'd rubbed that night so long ago without having a clue what she was doing.

He sucked the tender flesh into his mouth and an explosion of feeling rushed through her, starting between her thighs and sparking out like lightning through the rest of her body. She cried out in euphoria as his tongue caressed the area, making her skin pulse and her body jump.

Then Elena felt as if she were falling through a dark tunnel. Her head was spinning as her limbs dropped, feeling unimaginably heavy. The feeling continued on and on as he flicked out his tongue and made the sensation continue. It was long moments before she felt as if she were back on solid ground again.

She heard the unmistakable sound of a foil packet but she was too dazed to comprehend what that meant.

He climbed back up her body, his clothes still on — or so she thought.

He settled between her thighs and that's when she felt his thickness against her soaked opening.

"Look at me, Elena," he demanded. Her droopy eyelids slowly opened and the intensity of his gaze was almost too much for her to behold. "That's a good girl."

Her eyes flew open when he pushed forward, filling her with a hard thrust that stretched her opening and immediately made moisture and desire all converse to one specific spot.

Grabbing her hip, he angled her body and then pulled back before slamming forward again, this time harder and deeper. Her mouth widened in a blissful gasp as he continued thrusting in and out of her.

She groaned again, but this time, he captured the sound as he leaned down and took her lips, his tongue sinking into her mouth in a rhythm similar to the pace he kept as he moved in and out of her.

Pressure built and she cried out as she latched onto his thick shoulders.

"Come with me right now, Elena," he demanded.

Her eyes opened and she looked into his scorching gaze as her body responded to his powerful tone. She let go and flew even higher than when his mouth had worked magic between her thighs.

He groaned as he pressed tight inside her, and she felt his thickness pulsing against her sensitive walls.

Their breathing fogged the windows of the limo and he quickly sat up, adjusting his clothing, which was barely out of place, leaving her lying there with nothing on her but a sheen of damp sweat.

Finally she was able to move, and she sat up, pulling her clothing back on as quickly as her trembling fingers would allow. He still said nothing.

She began to fidget as she got the last of her clothes on, wondering what she'd done wrong. That had been the single most incredible experience of her life, but he seemed utterly unfazed.

Elena suddenly felt like crying. She didn't know why. It wasn't as if she'd had good sexual experiences so far. What did it matter what this man thought of her? She'd never cared what Leo thought . . .

"You are quite obedient," he finally said.

When she turned she found him looking directly at her. She wondered how long he'd been staring and how she hadn't felt his gaze boring into her.

"I . . ." She trailed off, not knowing what to say to that.

"I thought one time would be enough," he said, almost looking confused. "Obviously I was wrong. That's something that doesn't happen too often."

She was silent as he continued staring at her, the sign of possession in his eyes almost too much for her to bear. This was a look she hadn't witnessed before. It was a look she couldn't comprehend.

"Don't you have anything to say?" he finally asked.

She was silent a few more heartbeats before meeting his gaze. "I don't know what you expect from me," she finally muttered.

"Tell me you enjoyed what happened." Those words were certainly a command.

She refused to respond. He obviously didn't need his ego stroked. He had a big enough one for the entire state of Washington, obviously.

"I can make you tell me how you feel," he said with no inflection in his voice.

"You can't make me do anything," she said, feeling a slight buildup of her earlier defiance.

The grin that overtook his features told her she'd said exactly what he wanted.

Lightning fast, his hands reached out and she found herself facedown over his lap while his hand caressed her backside in a swirling motion.

"Oh, Elena, you are so not what I was expecting. I've decided I'm done being patient with you. Before this night is out you will tell me all I want to know, and you will do whatever I want."

She faced the seat, her anger rising as he continued stroking her ass. She hated him so much at this moment because the touch of his hand on her covered skin was making her wet again, making her feel those stirrings in her stomach.

Was it possible to feel desire and hate at the same time? Apparently so.

"Go to hell, Dalton," she whispered.

His hand moved from her ass and she thought he was beginning to take the hint. That was before it returned, this time not in a caress though, this time in a slapping downward motion that left a sting where he'd hit.

She was so shocked, her mouth gaped open and she tried to struggle to get away. His one arm didn't budge, holding her in place as his hand came down again, hitting her other cheek, leaving a sting where he'd slapped her.

Elena had been beaten, raped, and terrorized and had felt only fear. This fear was so much worse than any of those times, though, because even as his hand came down one more time, making her cry out, it wasn't pain that was filling her.

No, this was worse than those beatings, because as his hand slid beneath her, still leaving her pinned against him, and reached into her pants, it only took a few strokes of his hard finger against her dripping wet core and she came even harder than when he'd been buried deep inside her.

Tears fell down her face at the humiliation of how much she wanted this man, how much control he had over her. It was so different than anything she'd experienced so far, and she felt her world was spinning even more out of control.

He sat her up, this time her legs straddling his as he gripped her waist and looked into her eyes. There were questions in his gaze, and she wanted to turn away, but couldn't.

"Yes, Elena, I'm done playing," he said before lifting a hand and rubbing a piece of her hair back from her cheek. "You will tell me what I want to know."

She trembled in his arms but didn't say anything. The car stopped and he smiled at her. It was a predator's smile, a victor's smile. It was a smile that told her there was nothing she could do to stop this — to fight him *and* herself.

The door opened and she waited. She wasn't sure what would come next.

CHAPTER FORTY

"RETURN HER TO her room," Dalton said before walking away from the car, disappearing in a flash.

"This way, Elena," Lincoln said as he held the car door open for her.

"And if I refuse to follow you?" she asked, only the slightest tremble to her lip.

He was quiet for a moment as he looked at her. If she didn't know better she would think it was respect she was seeing in his expression. But Elena did know better. That couldn't possibly be what she was reading in his eyes.

"Then I would help you to change your mind," he answered.

A shiver ran through Elena as he said these words so nonchalantly. It didn't seem to be a threat exactly, but he'd been told to return her to her room, and that's exactly what he was going to do — any means necessary.

She hung her head the slightest bit and began to move toward the house. A movement down the driveway caught her eyes and she saw a reflection of what appeared to be a pair of eyes looking at her through the bushes.

A shudder passed through her and suddenly she picked up her pace, wanting to be anywhere other than outside in the lighted driveway. There were just too many shadows beyond the area they were currently in.

Lincoln said nothing else as the two of them made their way inside. She slowed down when she reached the huge staircase that would take her back to her prison. She really couldn't complain — it wasn't the worst of accommodations.

Stepping into the room, the finality of the door clicking shut behind her, the lock going into place, reminded her that she wasn't free to do whatever she wanted.

Elena noticed a tray of food sitting on the corner table in the room. Although she was hungry she was too frustrated to even think about eating. That moment of freedom as she ran down the windy beach had been the only joy she could ever remember feeling.

Now that she'd had a taste of it, she wanted more — so much more. She wanted to run and laugh and be able to make choices for herself. She wanted to outrun the horrible past of what her life was.

Elena walked over to the patio doors leading to the balcony and turned the knob, surprised when it opened. It hadn't been unlocked the entire time she'd been up in her current prison; she had still tried several times a day to get outside.

When the cool air hit her face from the safety of the second-story enclosed balcony, she felt as if she could finally take her first real breath since being taken so passionately in the back of that limo.

When she heard the door to her room unlocking, she tensed, but she knew whatever was to happen would happen. She couldn't fight any of this any more than she could fight a wild animal.

It was silent for several moments, but she was more than aware of his presence. It didn't take long for him to come and stand directly behind her, his hands coming up to rest on the rails on either side of her body, trapping her between him and the safety of the patio fencing.

The feel of his hot breath against her neck sent a shudder through her — but it wasn't unpleasant. How she wished that it was. Elena would love if she were just as repulsed by this man as she was by Leo.

One hand remained on the railing while the other one moved to her stomach and glided up the underside of her shirt while his lips made contact with her neck and he pushed against her, his erection very evident as he pressed against her backside.

When his hand glided over the swell of her breast and squeezed, his mouth opened and sucked at the skin of her neck; she couldn't stop the moan of pleasure from escaping.

"Sir, I'm going to leave now," Lincoln called from her room. Elena's body tensed in mortification. She'd thought they were alone.

Before Dalton could respond, Elena heard a sound below and then her body shook when she met the eyes of Leo, who was standing in the yard looking up at her with such venom, she knew he was now going to kill her. There was no longer any doubt.

He had to have seen the pleasure on her face as Dalton touched her. She might not like wanting Dalton, but she did indeed want him, and in a way she had never responded to Leo. The man below them was more than furious, and she would pay for what he would see as cheating. Her breath hitched.

That's when she noticed that Dalton, still pressed against her, was suddenly a statue. She couldn't even feel his breath on her neck anymore, though he hadn't pulled back yet. That didn't last long though.

Suddenly she felt herself spinning around, and his gaze was boring into hers. She was more terrified of the look in Dalton's eyes right now than anything she'd seen on Leo's face.

Without her saying a word, Elena had no doubt whatsoever that Dalton now knew it was Leo who had been raping and beating her. He pulled back, a low growl in his throat.

She was rooted to the spot.

What if Dalton went after Leo and he got away? She knew he would assume she'd told Dalton everything. She didn't see this ending well for her no matter which way the situation was to go. Fear made her eyes fill with tears.

"I'm going to kill him," Dalton said in such a low rumble she was frozen in place when he stepped away from her.

Dalton walked to the door and called the guard in. "Stay with her. Lincoln, you come with me. We have business to take care of."

Elena snapped out of her frozen state and rushed forward.

"No, Dalton, don't," she gasped, grabbing his arm.

He looked at her grip, terror freezing her to the spot. She had really screwed up this time. No matter what happened she would be the only loser.

"Stay inside this room, Elena," he growled, unclasping her fingers and handing her off to the guard who awaited her.

Dalton began walking toward the door, and Elena panicked. She freed herself from the guard and caught him before he made it halfway to her door. Not even thinking, she jumped on Dalton's back, making him stop in his tracks again and making Lincoln look at her in shock.

"Thanks for the help, buddy," Dalton told the man with sarcasm. Lincoln hadn't moved an inch.

"Do you really need help with a hundred pound woman?" Lincoln asked, his lips lifting the slightest bit, and a sparkle popping into his eyes.

Dalton glared at him, but he easily got Elena off his back. "What in the hell are you doing?" He didn't seem as angry as he had a moment ago, but still, his brows were raised.

"I don't want you to leave," she said, not able to think of a single other excuse.

"I'll definitely be back," he told her. "I have business to attend to first." He physically carried her over to the guard; the man apologizing profusely.

"Can you hold on to her this time?" Dalton snapped.

"Yes, sir, I'm sorry." The man was red in the face as he grabbed Elena. "Don't hurt her." Dalton's terse words seemed to make the man's face even redder.

He held on tightly, and Elena watched as Dalton and Lincoln walked from the room.

"Let me go," she cried out to the man who was solid as a board and not even grunting beneath her struggles.

"Are you going to try to leave the room again?" he asked, his arms not loosening.

"No! Just let me go," she demanded.

His arms loosened, but he quickly moved so he was blocking her bedroom door. Elena glared at him before swiveling around and marching back to the patio doors, slipping outside. She could hear the guard quickly approaching.

"Leave me alone," she whispered harshly as he stood behind her.

He had to already know this deck had no exit unless she planned on jumping. Of course he was only a couple feet away, most likely thinking that's exactly what she was going to do, and he wasn't going to let it happen.

She heard the voices before she found where they were coming from. She leaned over the railing, which earned her a tug from the guard on the top of her arm.

"I'm not going to jump," she snapped at him.

He didn't let her go. But he also didn't try to pull her away from her viewing spot.

Leo was standing in the corner of the yard with Dalton quickly approaching, Lincoln on his right side.

"Hey boss," Leo said, but she could hear the slight hint of menace in his voice.

Elena wasn't sure if Dalton heard the same thing or not. But without slowing his pace, he reached the man, and his arm came up and suddenly blood was squirting from the corner of Leo's mouth and dripping from his nose.

"What the hell?" Leo shouted as he staggered on his feet but didn't go down.

"You're the one Elena is afraid of. You're the one who has left her bruised and I'm sure so much more," Dalton said, his voice cold as ice.

Leo's eyes widened before he jerked his hate-filled eyes in her direction and then spit blood out to the ground.

"I've done nothing your family hasn't demanded I do," Leo snapped.

Dalton did show a reaction to this, which might have bolstered Leo's confidence.

"Your sick bastard of a father had us kidnap all sorts of girls. Elena normally would have been too old for the perv, at almost seventeen, what with training time and all, but she was a real treat — even back then," Leo said with a laugh. "Besides, this wasn't just any kidnapping was it, Dalton? No, this one was for hire."

Elena couldn't tell what Dalton was thinking about all of this because he didn't show the slightest reaction. She, however, was rooted to the spot. Kidnapped? What was he talking about? She knew she was a prisoner here? But they'd told her she was a runaway.

"I'm not my father, and I told you there would be no abuse here," Dalton finally said. "I also don't owe you a damn explanation."

A shiver traveled down Elena's spine. If Dalton spoke to her in that voice she would quickly heed to whatever it was he was commanding of her. There was power in his tone, but Leo didn't seem to be picking up on it.

"You knew what was going on," Leo thundered. "Just because you wear your fancy expensive suits and watches that cost more than some people's houses doesn't mean you're above the law. You kept the bitch even after your father died, and from what I've seen, you're following in daddy's footsteps." Leo spit at the ground again, this time the blood and mucus almost landing on Dalton's shoe.

Apparently Dalton was done. Before the man knew what was happening, Dalton attacked, punching him over and over again, blood splattering against him and the ground.

Elena couldn't move as the man who had caused her so much pain was being beaten to death. Even after Leo was crumpled before him, Dalton continued to pound his fists against him.

"It's time to go in," the guard said as if just realizing that maybe she shouldn't watch this.

"No!" she screamed at the man.

Her voice must have done something because midair, Dalton's fist dropped as he turned his head and found her standing there, staring down at the mess.

He turned away and looked at Lincoln before grabbing a handkerchief and wiping blood from his face.

Leo lay there motionless in a bloody heap, his nose and jaw obviously broken.

"Get this filthy piece of trash off my property. You know what to do," Dalton said to Lincoln who nodded at him.

He then looked back up at her, and Elena decided she'd seen enough. What had Leo been talking about? She wanted answers, but she didn't know how to get them. The one person who appeared to know who she really was wouldn't be talking to anyone anytime soon — or more likely, anytime ever again.

She moved over to her bed and fell onto it. She barely breathed as she waited for Dalton to come back to her. And she knew he would very soon.

When the door opened and shut again less than ten seconds later, she knew Dalton was with her and the guard was gone. She didn't turn to look at him.

"Why didn't you tell me?" he asked, fury still clear in his eyes.

"I knew if I did that Leo would kill me," she said, no emotion in her voice.

"I would have protected you — I still will," he thundered.

"Really, Dalton?" she screamed as she shot up in bed. "Because I don't know anything anymore. I don't know who I am. I don't know how I got here, and I don't trust you."

She was panting hard as his eyes narrowed, and he stepped closer to her.

"You don't want to know who you really are," he warned her.

The conviction in his voice and eyes as he said that made her think she might not want to know. Fear was racing through her, and she wondered if she would be okay not to know.

"I deserve to know," she finally said, trying not to back down from him.

But when he took another step closer to her, she knew this wasn't a battle she was going to win — she'd never had a chance of winning.

"You should have told me," he said, his tone so deadly it made her shake.

"I . . . I don't know what you want from me, Dalton," she gasped when she found her voice again.

"I want the damn truth, Elena!" he thundered.

"I don't have a right to tell the truth!" she said, her temper coming back even though she was still terrified.

"What in the hell is that supposed to mean?"

"You own me, Dalton, and everyone knows it. I don't know who I am, what I am, *why* I'm here, but anyone and everyone can do whatever they want with me, including *you*, so why are you so mad that I'm not ratting out every little thing that happens to me? Why is it that this is what pisses you off so much?" she snapped.

He stopped his pursuit only inches away from her as his eyes narrowed even more. And then he ignored most of her speech, focusing only on a few short words she would forever regret saying.

"I own you?" he asked, his voice deceptively calm.

She decided she'd said enough. She didn't back away because the bed was right behind her. She had nowhere to go. Maybe jumping from that balcony wouldn't be the worst thing she could do tonight. She wondered about her chance of actually making it there.

It was slim to none.

"If you want to be owned, I'll show you exactly how that feels," he told her.

Gripping her arm, he then pushed her backward onto the bed and reached for his tie. Elena couldn't breathe as she looked at this man with eyes of steel.

Had she just made her life a hell of a lot worse? Was Dalton her savior or was he the one she needed saved from?

Manufactured by Amazon.ca
Acheson, AB